The Starting Five

Felicia Taylor

DEDICATION

I would like to dedicate this book to my children, Chris, Devin, Ashely, and Christopher.

I would also like to dedicate this book to my parents, Vivian (aka) Lady "V" and Rodney (aka) "Cool."

Rest in Heaven. I miss you guys so much.

CONTENTS

ACKNOWLEDGMENTS

First and foremost, my family. Everybody knows how I feel about my family. Thank all of you guys for believing in me. It means everything.

To my son Devin, thank you for always encouraging me to chase my dreams. To my sister-cousin Kelly, who jokingly called me Laitha Waithe one day. However, I knew that was just her way of encouraging me and letting me know that I could do anything I set my mind to.

Thank You to Ashley, Robyn, Shay, Ronnie, and Theresa, who often tell me how proud they are of me. That kept me going most days. Thank you to my brother Kevin, who always encourages me.

A special thank you goes to Mario, my babe, and rock. Your unwavering belief in my abilities has been a constant source of inspiration. Your daily reminders that I can achieve anything I set my mind to have fueled my determination to see this book through. Thank you for always being my number-one supporter.

Please note this work of fiction is intended solely for entertainment purposes. It explores the realm of imagination and allows for the creation and development of characters and stories. While there may be subtle references and metaphors related to personal experiences and anxiety, it's my hope that my family will be able to interpret and connect with these elements.

Once again, to everyone mentioned and countless others who have touched my life, thank you from the bottom of my heart. Your support has meant everything to me.

PROLOGUE/FOREWORD

We all know the saying, "What goes around, comes around," right? And for those who don't, you will after this prologue. Now, I don't know what it's like being a girl because I'm not one. But what I do know is y'all came to be real messy at times; I mean for no good reason, just messy!

Peep this, I'm gonna let you in on some shit that went down at my high school ten years ago. Who am I, you might ask? We'll get to that later. In the Lou, where I grew up (yeah, that's short for St. Louis, Missouri), known as the 'show me' state, there were all types of chicks back then. You had the popular girls, the mean girls, the tough girls, the smart girls, and the list goes on and on. But somehow, Brandy didn't fit in anywhere. She had a lot of struggles with her identity, often looking in the mirror and asking God, "Who am I? What am I?"

Afraid of facing social stigma, being labeled, harassed, or even discriminated against, she kept these struggles to herself. Besides, back then, you didn't talk about stuff like that at a black family dinner table. Once Brandy realized her family had her back, life was great!

Pops always said, "Family first!" And that was a phrase that became embedded in her spirit. She was unstoppable in her personal life, as well as on the basketball court. I'm telling y'all, she really had it going on. Everything was good until the fall of 2010, during the championship game, homecoming week, and fourth quarter. That's when shit hit the fan.

CHAPTER 1

The grey gym doors swung open, eager students filling the bleachers representing their schools' colors: blue, yellow, burgundy, and gold. Roaring and cheering as the song "We're Playing Basketball" is being played, the familiar beats of the song blasted through the speakers, engulfing the gym in an energetic rhythm. The most highly anticipated game of the·year was underway in a matter of minutes, and the community had been eagerly waiting for this moment.

The Salem East Stingrays were about to face off against their fierce rivals, the Salem West Wildcats. Damn, this crowd was lit, clapping and stomping along to the catchy tune; you would have thought it was the NBA Finals. The head coaches, Lisa Underwood and Cheryle Thomas, led their teams onto the court and were met by frenzied reporters eager for a scoop. The girls hit the court, their bodies moving with lightning speed, twisting and turning in a dazzling display of athleticism, while the crowd serenaded them with a harmonious blend of emotions. The reporter blushed and flashed a smile at both coaches before diving into the interview.

"Ladies, I remember seeing you two balling together back in high school and college. Now, witnessing you as coaches is a true honor. You all played together for several years. How does it feel to compete at this level?" Coach Cheryle glanced at Lisa, a smile gracing her face, before addressing the reporter. She caressed her basketball, answering, "We always knew we'd end up right here. Lisa knows I love her like a play cousin, but this is basketball, baby!" She hyped up the crowd, raising her hands in the air, bursting with infectious enthusiasm. "Let's gooo!" The reporter playfully teased, "Ouch! Sounds like some basketball fighting words to me," the reporter chuckled, winking at Lisa. "I know you're not going to take that," he said.

1

Lisa took a moment to soak it all in, her heart swelling with pride, as this is familiar territory. Lisa cleared her throat and began to speak. "Returning to my alma mater, stepping foot on this court again where magic was made, fills me with immense pride. All I can say is, I hope they brought their A-game. Because we sure brought ours." Lisa bounced up and down, clapping her hands, an ear-to-ear grin spreading across her face. "LET'S GO STINGRAYS... WE GOT THIS!" she said. With that, the reporter bowed his head toward both ladies and thanked them for the interview. "Good luck, ladies," he said.

As the girls continued to warm up, the reporter tracked down a couple of students to interview. He approached the girl who was dancing and twerking first. "So, tell me, young lady, who do you think is going to win the championship game?" he asked in a firm voice. "I'm not sure. West is looking pretty good over there. They have Charlie and Frankie. Those girls are hard!" she replied.

The reporter then turned his head towards a young man and asked, "And who do you have?" The young man replied while taking off his snapback and scratching his head, "Man, I can't call it, but I'm representing East. Brandy's a beast!" "Great. Thanks, guys!" the reporter replied as he made his way to the Salem West Wildcats for a quick interview. The reporter then decided to speak to Charlie, the captain and point guard of the Salem West Wildcats.

"Charlie, I know you're the captain of the team, so I'll ask you this question. Everybody knows that the Salem West Wildcats are going for a 4-peat. Last year, it was McKinley High. The year before that, it was Truman. And the year before that, it was Marshall. Now, a 4-peat has never been accomplished on a high school level, but the Lakers had 4 straight wins under the leadership of Pat Riley. How have you guys prepared for this moment?" he said.

Charlie, flooded with emotions, answered with a touch of sadness on her face, "Unfortunately, I didn't attend Salem West my freshman year. But if we pull this off, it will be my third win and my girls' fourth," she said, smiling at her teammates. "And how did we prepare for this moment? Eat, sleep, basketball, repeat. That's how," she continued. "Thank you, Charlie, for that comment!" the reporter replied and took off.

After warming up for the game, the Salem West Wildcats stood on the sidelines, donning their Wildcats colors of blue and yellow. Charlene Morrison 'Charlie' (No.31), Althea Lewis 'Teddy' (No.32), Sundance McQuay

'Suni' (No.3), Francesca Cardona 'Frankie' (No.54), and Willow Stephenson 'Billie' (No.24) were all part of the Starting 5 lineup. The girls laughed and teased Brandy and her team as they warmed up. Teddy, looking over at Brandy and her girls, said, "Yo, we're about to put a whooping on Salem East!" "Yeah, for real! This game is going to be a breeze," Billie replied. Frankie, however, shook her head and replied, "I don't know. I wouldn't be so sure, Billie!" Charlie stood up, put her hands on her hips, stared at Brandy, and said, "Yeah, let's just hope Brandy isn't on her A-game." Suni jumped up, "The hell with Brandy! That thing doesn't even come close to us. We are the Starting 5! Or did you forget that, Charlie?" she replied.

Charlie started laughing and responded, "Yeah, you're right." Teddy turned to her teammates and said, "Besides, everybody came to see us!" She pointed to the gym floor. "This may not be our home court, but everybody knows what's up with us," she replied. The girls' facial expressions filled with disgust as the Salem East cheerleaders made their way in with the captain of the squad, Kameron, who happened to be a male cheerleader. Kameron noticed the girls staring at him and decided to approach them.

Standing tall at 5 feet 9 inches with a pierced nose, caramel skin, and a neatly trimmed short fade with frosted tips, he got up in Charlie's face and said, "What the hell are you looking at?" Charlie began laughing and looked back at her girls. "Yeah, that's what the hell we're standing here trying to figure out! So, what are you?" she replied. Smacking on his gum and popping bubbles, Kameron looked at Charlie bitterly and said, "I'm your worst nightmare, tramp!" At the same time, Teddy looked at Kameron and said, "Man, forget this he-she!" As they started to walk off, Kameron vigorously walked behind them and yelled out, "You know, you guys are prancing around here like this is your house. This isn't your house; it's Brandy's house!"

Teddy leaned an inch closer to Kameron's face and said, "Damn, dude, I'm confused. Are you a cheerleader for East or just Brandy's personal cheerleader?" "Don't worry about that! Just know Brandy is going to mop the floor with y'all's asses!" Kameron replied. Charlie abruptly turned around and said, "Oh yeah, we'll see about that!" As Brandy warmed up on the sideline with her teammates, her phone buzzed in her pocket. She retrieved it, quickly glancing at the screen to see her mother's name flashing across it. With a smile, she stepped aside to find a quiet spot away from the bustling gymnasium. "Hey, Mom," Brandy greeted warmly, her voice filled with affection. She told her mom, "I'll see you when you get here. Oh, and tell him I love him too," she said before hanging up the phone.

Brandy and her teammates were stretching on the sideline, preparing for the game, when Charlie and the Starting 5 approached them. Charlie could not resist the opportunity to taunt Brandy with a mischievous grin across her face. "You know, all that stretching won't help you on the court, right?" she said. There was a flicker in Brandy's eyes as she replied, "You scared, Charlie?" "Girl, bye! Nothing about you scares me! Please believe!" Charlie exclaimed. Suni joined in, cautioning, "Be careful when getting up; something might fall out of your shorts." The girls erupted in laughter, attempting to rattle Brandy's confidence.

However, Brandy's smile faded, and her expression turned somber. Her teammates noticed the change in her demeanor and gathered around her. "Hey Brandy, what was that all about?" Rivers asked. "Don't worry about them. Let's just make it count on the court," Brandy replied. Brandy's teammates helped her stand up, and they all proceeded to the locker room just a few minutes before the start of the game. While sitting in the locker room, Brandy looked dazed, rubbing the necklace around her neck, thinking about what Suni had said to her over and over. "Be careful when standing up; something might fall out of your shorts!" She tried to recall the exact words.

Meanwhile, Travis and his boy Deuce were sitting in the bleachers, watching Frankie and the rest of the girls warm up. Deuce bobbed his head back and forth to the music while brushing his fade. Deuce said, "Man, it's raining sexy honeys in here today. And you are incredibly lucky, my friend. Frankie is looking good." Travis smiled at Frankie as she warmed up and said to Deuce, "Yeah, I'm going to marry that girl!" Blushing and dancing in place, Deuce said to Travis, "Oh snap... that's wifey right there!" Dapping his boy as the girls walked into the locker room, Travis smiled and winked at Frankie as she passed by. Deuce said, "Man, this sure as hell beats looking at a bunch of sweaty dudes in the finals. Besides, you guys really sucked this year." Laughing and nodding his head, Travis replied, "So true." Dapping Deuce, he added, "So happy you guys won the football championship. I am proud of you, bro!"

Moments later, in the locker room, Brandy gathered her teammates for prayer before the game. Standing in their team colors, burgundy and gold, they embraced each other and said, "Amen!" Brandy raised her head, clapped her hands, and turned to her team. "The game is about to start. Let's block out the noise," she said, pointing towards the other locker room. "Let's get this win!" Brandy walked to the exit of the locker room. Teddy noticed Brandy coming out and gently touched Charlie. Charlie looked at Brandy and nodded, saying, "Yeah, it's on, tramp!" Frankie had a look of disgust on her face, showing disapproval. "Why do you have to be so mean, Charlie?"

Frankie said. "Frankie, shut up! Whose side are you on anyway?" Suni added. "The right side!" Frankie responded. Billie turned to her teammates and said, "Come on, girls. Let's not lose focus! Let's go."

Meanwhile, Jessica and Keshawn, both Salem West and Salem East commentators, were discussing their predictions for today's game. Looking all around at the crowd and waving, most of them being her teammates, Jessica made this statement, "I don't know what's about to happen, but one thing is for sure, this crowd is lit." "Yeah, as far as I am concerned, there are no losers," Keshawn replied. Nodding her head, Jessica replied, "Facts!" The lights were turned down low, and the gym was packed.

An announcer with a deep voice came on the loudspeaker to announce the teams. The announcer said, "Ladies and gentlemen, boys and girls, please welcome to the floor, all the way from the WEST SIDE!!! Give it up for the SALEM WESTT WILDDDD CATSSSS!!!" The crowd erupted in loud cheers as the Salem West Wildcats came through the double doors into the gym. The announcer then introduced the home team. "And now, I need you to show some love for the home team, the Salem East STIIIIING RAYYYS!" The Salem East Stingrays emerged from the tunnel. The crowd erupted into cheers, the atmosphere was electric, and the upbeat rhythm of 'Whose House' by RUN DMC filled the gym, intensifying the anticipation.

The players emerged one by one from the tunnel, their jerseys shining brightly under the spotlight. The crowd went crazy as the girls from both teams made their way onto the court. Before the game started, both coaches decided to have sidebars with their teams. Coach Cheryle had a talk with her Wildcats before the game. "Alright, guys, today is your time! Let's get this win. Let's show everyone who we are. On me, 1, 2, 3, Wildcats!" Coach Lisa Underwood had a sidebar with her Stingrays. She stood there, visibly emotional, as tears filled her eyes. She chuckled and said, "I guess if I were to say that you guys didn't know how personal this is for me, I would be lying, right?!" She chuckled. "You girls are the number one basketball team in the state, so it's only right if you guys won today." The girls looked at her and shook their heads. "Yes, coach, we know. We got you," Brandy replied. Coach Lisa wiped her tears and said, "Enough said! Let's do what we're here to do." Coach Lisa looked at Brandy, who had a determined look on her face. "Okay, hands in!" All the girls put their hands in the middle of the circle. "1, 2, 3, Stingrays!" they shouted.

Players from each team took their positions, and the referee tossed the ball. Alexander faced off with Morrison in the center of the court for the jump, with the referee in between them. He put his whistle between his lips and blew it as he threw the ball up. Both Alexander and Morrison jumped to catch the ball, but Morrison won the tip-off and sent the ball back to McQuay, who caught it and passed it back to Morrison, who was behind her. Once Charlie had the ball, they began to run up the court to the Stingrays' side. Morrison stepped on the 3-point line. Morrison was closely guarded by Alexander, but that didn't faze her as she raised her arms, shot the ball, and it went in, touching nothing but the net. Morrison pumped her fist in excitement, then ran back up the court as the Stingrays got hold of the ball.

Alexander, who now had the ball, dribbled it down the court to the left side. She stopped on the 3-point line and was very closely guarded by Morrison. Alexander was trapped because not only was Morrison tightly guarding her, but she also towered above her by a few inches. A slight smile came on Alexander's face as if she had a plan. She raised her hand and faked the ball, which made Morrison raise her arm to block the ball and turn around. While Morrison looked away, Alexander took the advantage to shoot the ball. And just like Morrison, SWOOSH, the shot was nothing but net. The score was tied with both teams at 3. The crowd was going wild. Morrison turned around to Alexander with a scowl on her face. Alexander looked into Morrison's eyes with the most intimidating look, threw her hands up, and said, "What?" Alexander ran up the court, and McQuay and Lewis came up to Morrison. Charlie was steaming. "So, if this is how she wants to play... Let's play."

Morrison and McQuay ran up the court while Lewis went back and retrieved the ball from Cardona, who stood outside the court, ready to pass the ball to Lewis. In a montage scene, Alexander and Morrison went back and forth, making nothing but clean shots and fouls on both sides. Morrison intentionally fouled Alexander with an elbow to the face. Lewis dunked, and both Stephenson and Alexander got a defensive rebound. The score was 15-10 in the first quarter, with the Stingrays taking the lead. The second quarter began, and the atmosphere in the gym was electric. The game between the Stingrays and their rivals was in full swing. The Wildcats had a slight lead, with the score 30-26 in their favor. Kameron cheered on the sideline as the crowd went crazy. As the second quarter ended, the Wildcats were still in the lead, with the score being 75-60. On the sideline, the coaches rallied their players during halftime for a pep talk.

As halftime ended, the Stingrays huddled together, their determination evident on their faces. They listened attentively to Coach Lisa Underwood, absorbing her every word. The crowd was lit, with roars and cheers echoing throughout the gym, setting the stage for an exhilarating second half. The Wildcats' captain, Charlene Morrison, and the Stingrays' captain, Brandy

Alexander, locked eyes, both fueled by the desire to emerge victorious. The tone was set for an intense battle that would keep the crowd on their feet until the final buzzer sounded.

In the third quarter, the Wildcats lost their momentum as their shots barely connected to the hoop. Coach Cheryle Thomas became frustrated. The third quarter ended with a score of 75-62, and the Stingrays took the lead.

The fourth quarter started, and the Stingrays continued to excel, making shots and blocking their opponents. Time quickly wound down, and in the final seconds of the game, the score was tied at 93-93. The Stingrays had the ball with 1.1 seconds left. Rivers passed the ball to Alexander, who leaped into the air, her body fully extended, and released the ball with a flick of her wrist. Time seemed to stand still as the basketball sailed through the air, arcing gracefully toward the hoop. The entire gymnasium held its breath. And then, with a resounding swish, the ball effortlessly dropped through the net at the buzzer. The Stingrays won the championship with a score of 96-93.

Brandy kissed the necklace around her neck as she landed on the court, her legs giving way beneath her as a surge of overwhelming emotion washed over her. Tears of joy streamed down her face, blending with the sweat that adorned her brow. She collapsed onto her knees, her body shaking with the weight of the moment. The crowd exploded into a frenzy, their cheers blending with her cries of elation.

Coach Lisa, standing on the sidelines, watched the scene unfold with a mix of pride and awe. Brandy's eyes locked with hers, and she knew that this moment was more than just a victory for the team—it was a testament to their shared journey of hard work, dedication, and trust. A smile played on Coach Lisa's lips, her eyes glistening with tears. They nodded at each other, their gestures filled with respect and admiration. Pointing at each other, they silently conveyed their shared victory, recognizing that this championship was a culmination of their combined efforts.

The crowd was roaring as Brandy's teammates embraced her. Crying tears of joy, she walked up to the reporter as her team and school cheered her on for bringing home the victory for the Stingrays. Taking the end of her jersey to wipe the sweat off her head, she stood next to the reporter, taking it all in as the crowd yelled, "MVP! MVP!"

The Wildcats stood on the court, their faces filled with anger and disappointment. Frankie from the Wildcats stepped forward. "Come on, guys," Frankie said. "It's not the end of the world. We fought hard, and we gave it everything we had. Let's go congratulate them." Moments later, the starting 5 from the Wildcats approached Brandy to congratulate her, or at least that is what she thought.

Frankie came over to congratulate Brandy on her victory. She tapped her gently on the shoulder, catching her attention amid the post-game chaos. "Congratulations, Brandy!" Frankie said. "Girl, you played an incredible game. Much respect." Brandy turned towards Frankie, a radiant smile spreading across her face as she nodded appreciatively. "Thank you, Frankie," Brandy replied.

Brandy tried to focus on the interview. However, she became suspicious because the remaining four girls were whispering to one another. Not knowing what was about to happen, Brandy turned around to talk to the reporter, and that is when it happened. The remaining four girls grabbed Brandy's shorts, pulling them down to her knees. The crowd let out a gasp, and Charlie turned around to the crowd and said, "She ain't who she said she is, y'all."

All cheering came to a halt. Some kids started laughing and pointing, while others stood in shock. Someone even yelled out, "OMG, she has a penis!" Some started crying because they were Brandy's friends. Kameron, grabbing his head in disbelief, yelled out to Charlie, "Why would you do this?" Frankie turned around to her teammates, screaming, "That's messed up, Charlie!" Brandy started to cry as she did a 180 around the whole gym, looking at the kids, with some of them looking at her with disgust. She pulled her pants up and ran out of the gym. Kameron cried as Brandy ran out, and he took off running after her but was stopped by Frankie and both coaches. "No, I got it!" Frankie stated and took off after Brandy.

Watching her run out of the gym crying, Kameron stood there, looking at Charlie. "She didn't deserve this! And you know it!" he said before he took off running. Frankie ran out of the gym, looking to her right and then to her left. She spotted Brandy running up the steps. "Brandy!" she yelled and took off after her. Frankie ran up the steps as fast as she could, her legs growing heavier with each step, but she refused to give up. She took her time, checking all three floors for Brandy, yelling her name, but there was no response. Frankie stopped for a minute to catch her breath. However, she noticed there was one more flight of steps to climb and was determined to make her way to the top. Frankie continued yelling Brandy's name.

Finally, she arrived at the top of the staircase, but Brandy was nowhere to be found. Forcing air out of her lungs, she yelled Brandy's name one more time, but once again, there was no response. Frankie stood in place, resting her hands on her hips as she desperately tried to catch her breath. Her focus shifted to a flickering light coming from a nearby window. Frankie felt a sudden urge to approach the window. She took tentative steps towards the window, the light growing stronger with each passing moment. As she reached the window, she pressed her trembling hands against the cool glass. Her eyes widened with horror at the sight that greeted her.

Brandy stood on the narrow ledge of the school building. Frankie let out a piercing scream. "NO!!! NO!" A surge of adrenaline coursed through Frankie's veins, propelling her into action.

Frankie's eyes scanned her surroundings as she searched from the door to the rooftop. Her heart pounded in her chest as she burst through the heavy doors. "Brandy! Stop!" she screamed. With each step, Frankie's voice grew louder, her plea filled with raw emotion. "Brandy, don't do this! You're not alone! We can face this together. I'm so sorry this happened to you. I promise I had nothing to do with this. Please, just come back from the edge." Frankie closed the distance, her hand reaching out towards Brandy. "Take my hand, Brandy," she pleaded.

Meanwhile, as Frankie continued pleading with Brandy, the other four girls, Kameron, both coaches, the principal, along with an abundance of students, made their way to the rooftop. Billie saw Brandy and screamed out, "What the hell!"

Without thinking, Kameron ran towards Brandy, but she stopped him. "Kam, I love you, and I'm sorry. Please do not come any closer," she stated, crying. "I love you too, Brandy. Please come down," Kameron pleaded. Whispers floated through the air, filled with disbelief and sorrow. Some students couldn't bear to watch, turning their heads away, while others remained rooted to the spot, their eyes locked on Brandy as if willing her to find the strength to step back. The tension on the rooftop was palpable as Brandy stood on the ledge, her tear-streaked face a mirror of anguish. Her eyes fixed on Charlie, who stood a few feet away. Brandy's voice quivered as she spoke, her words laced with hurt. Crying, she asked, "You hate me that much, Charlie?" Charlie replied, "I don't know what the hell you're talking about." Brandy stated, "You know!" Suni shook her head. "Hold up! You know this freak, Charlie?" Billie asked. Brandy shrugged her shoulders. "I don't deserve this," Brandy stated.

Charlie stared at Brandy and made this statement, "You're sick, and you need help," chuckling. Shaking her head and wiping her tears, Brandy replied, "No, you're sick." Billie grabbed Charlie by the arm and said, "No, wait, y'all know each other?" Frankie continued to plead with Brandy to come down. "Y'all, please do something. Help her!" Teddy stood up and said, pointing at Brandy, "Now, wait a minute, didn't nobody tell her ass to get up there?" With a trembling voice, Brandy turned to Charlie and said, "Charlie, go ahead, tell them why you hate me." Charlie replied, "You're a fucking liar!" Charlie walked towards the ledge, and Frankie grabbed her arm. Charlie yanked away from Frankie. "Do it, I dare you," Charlie said, smirking at Brandy. "Are you crazy?" Frankie replied. Frankie continued pleading with Brandy, "No, please don't do this. Charlie, please help." Charlie finally relented. "Alright, alright. Look, we're sorry, okay? You don't want to do this. It ain't that serious," she replied.

The crowd grew bigger and bigger as Brandy stood on the ledge. She looked down at her necklace, kissed it, and said, "'SORRY B.'" Kameron ran towards Brandy, attempting to grab her, but was unsuccessful and screamed as Brandy hit the ground. The crowd gathered in front of the school, where Brandy's body lay in a puddle of blood, but they were stopped by the police officers and crime scene tape. A lady arrived at the school, pushing her way through the crowd. "Hey, Kameron, what's going on here?" she asked. Kameron was crying hysterically. The lady grabbed Kameron by the face and asked again. "Mrs. Alexander, it's Brandy," he replied. Brandy's mother began busting her way to get to Brandy, and the police officer, caught off guard by Brandy's mother's determination, reached out to grab her and hold her back.

But fueled by a mother's love and desperation, she pushed their weight aside, determined to reach her injured daughter. Ignoring the pain in her own heart, Brandy's mother rushed to her daughter's side, tripping and stumbling on her way. Her hands trembled as she cradled Brandy's broken body, the blood staining her clothes. Brandy's mother's voice filled with sorrow and disbelief. "Not my baby. Why, God? Why?" Her gut-wrenching scream echoed through the courtyard, a raw expression of a mother's anguish and confusion. The students, previously stunned into silence, now found their own tears streaming down their faces, their hearts breaking for Brandy and her devastated mother. The police officers, realizing the futility of trying to hold Brandy's mother back, shifted their focus to consoling her gently, their voices filled with empathy and understanding. We'll find out what happened, ma'am. Please try to stay strong."

The scene faded out, leaving a palpable sense of sorrow and uncertainty hanging over the school as the community came to terms with the devastating event that had unfolded before their eyes. On this rainy day, an unknown person sat in a dimly lit room, their eyes fixed on the television screen broadcasting the latest news of how Brandy Alexander committed suicide while burning a picture of the Starting 5 newspaper clipping. The news anchor came on and said, "Promising student Brandy Alexander of Missouri, also known by her community as the Beast, a name she wore like a badge of honor, took her own life yesterday after being humiliated by a group of girls during a high school basketball championship game."

Brandy was scheduled for a Vaginoplasty and Phalloplasty, also known as bottom surgery, this spring. Friends and family described Brandy as a sweet and kind human being. Brandy wanted to be a doctor. She was also recruited to play for the Michigan State Spartans women's basketball team. It is unclear why the student was targeted, but one thing we do know is another rising star is gone too soon. As the news report unfolded, Brandy's picture appeared on the television.

The unknown person's breath became heavier, reflecting a mixture of frustration and resentment driven by a surge of anger. They stormed over to a nearby table where an empty bottle of liquor lay. Their hands gripped the bottle tightly, their knuckles turning ashy under strain, and in a fit of rage, they flung it towards the television screen with all their might. The glass shattered on impact, blowing out the screen. On this rainy day, a person of interest in a hoodie approached Brandy's gravesite. The person bent over and placed flowers on Brandy's grave. The song "Giving Up" played as the person walked away.

CHAPTER 2

Fast forward 10 years, Travis, a 6-foot-tall man with smooth caramel skin and curly hair, found himself standing at the bottom of the hill in a sleek black suit tailored to perfection. As he wiped the car windows, waiting for Frankie to emerge from the house, the sun bathed the neighborhood. Travis caught sight of his beautiful wife walking down the porch. Her presence radiated captivating elegance that seemed to transcend time.

She wore a cream-colored fitted dress that beautifully accentuated her graceful curves, and her long hair cascaded in waves, elegantly secured in a chic side ponytail. The passing years had only enhanced her natural beauty. "Damn, baby, you look absolutely stunning. The bride won't have anything on you," Travis whispered, unable to contain his admiration. A wide smile adorned Frankie's face, her eyes shimmering with love and contentment. She approached the car with a graceful stride, exuding a quiet confidence that could only be formed through years of shared experiences.

Travis closes Frankie's car door after she gets into the passenger seat. He then walks around to the driver's seat and gets in. Travis looked at Frankie and could tell she had some reservations about the wedding.

"It's been a long time. Are you ready, baby?" he asked with a wink. She looks at her man with a smile and replies, "Yes, my king."

He then proceeds to turn the key in the ignition, turn up the volume on his Bluetooth, adjust his mirror, and push his shades up on his face. "Let's get it!" he says to Frankie as the song "Ain't No Woman Like the One I Got" starts playing. The drive is smooth, the car gliding along the asphalt with a quiet efficiency that makes Frankie feel relaxed and content.

One hour later, Frankie and Travis arrive at Cooper's Banquet Hall, where the wedding and reception are taking place. Travis turns off the car and looks over at Frankie, who is breathing heavily. As they make their way to the wedding venue, Travis takes Frankie's hands and says, "Listen, baby, you don't have to do this. Just say the word, and I will turn this car on and head home." Frankie replies, "No, it's okay, babe. I'm ready." Travis responds with a smile, saying, "That's my girl! Baby, I'm telling you, when God made you, he broke the mold." Frankie blushes and replies, "Thank you, babe."

Frankie and Travis both get out of the car and head toward the venue, looking back at the car and smiling. "Hmm... valet parking, that's nice," Frankie states. "Yeah, it's a'ight," Travis replies, chuckling. Travis takes Frankie by the hand and says, "Come on, baby," as they head up the hill to the Majestic Hall, where the wedding is going to take place.

Frankie stops at the door, and Travis waits, saying, "Baby, just breathe. You've got this, and I've got you!" She nods her head with a smile at Travis and says, "Okay." Frankie looks to her side at her man and takes one last breath as she grabs both handles on the marble door and pulls them open. When Frankie opens the door and steps inside the church, there is a loud gasp! People are looking as if they've seen a ghost.

Frankie becomes nervous and whispers under her breath to Travis, "Everyone is staring at me! Why is everyone staring at me?" Travis replies, "Because you're the finest woman in here, shit! That's why. Now let's find us some seats." People in the church continue to stare in awe as the couple searches for a place to sit. Someone in the pew even yells out, "Hey, look, it's Frankie!" A couple of Frankie and Travis's high school classmates, Marly and Tyreke, make a statement, "Yeah, it sure is," as they point and smile at the same time.

Tyreke says, "Man, she's still fine as hell!" Marly retorts, "Haha, and your ass is still married, so ha-ha that!" Tyreke responds in a playful tone, "Oh, come on, baby, you know nobody is as fine as you." Marly replies, "Yeah, right!"

Travis approaches a couple sitting at the end of one of the pews and says, "Excuse me, are these seats taken?" The gentleman replies, "No, they're not." Taking Frankie by the arm, Travis says, "Come on, baby, let's sit here." Frankie replies, "Sounds good, babe."

Clapping her hands at the wedding party, who are all lined up in the hall, waiting to go inside, Millie, the wedding coordinator, stands at 5 feet 10 inches tall, with a slender build, brown caramel skin, brown curly hair tied in a bun, and glasses. She addresses the group, her voice carrying a touch of humor and a hint of authority.

"Now, ladies, make sure your dresses are wrinkle-free," Millie said, her eyes sweeping over the women. "Every detail matters, from your neatly fixed hair to the careful arrangement of your dresses." Millie glanced over at Teddy, who stood there in a beautiful indigo blue bridesmaid dress with a short fiery red bald fade, a look of disgust on her face, before returning her gaze to the rest of the ladies. "Let's ensure that our attire mirrors the beauty of the occasion. Well... most of us anyway," she added sarcastically.

"Is that bitch throwing shade at me?" Teddy muttered. "Scoffs! I hope not. She doesn't want any of us," Suni replied. She then turned her gaze to the gentlemen, a twinkle in her eye.

"And gentlemen, tuck in your shirts, straighten your ties. Let the elegance of your attire be a testament to your presence here today," Millie continued. Teddy simply stared at Millie, wondering where the hell they found her. "She's annoying as hell!" Teddy exclaimed. "Tell me about it," Billie replied.

Mille looked at the group one last time and said, "Places, everyone! The wedding is about to begin."

Pastor Honeycutt entered the pulpit in a crisp white robe. "Shall we all rise?" he stated. "Let me say this before the wedding ceremony begins. The bride and groom ask if you could all silence your phones during the ceremony, and yes, pictures are allowed. However, they ask that you don't post any pictures on any social media platforms."

The wedding party stood in anticipation as the bride prepared to make her entrance down the aisle. The song "You" by R&B recording artist Jesse Taylor played, setting the mood. The processional order of the wedding began with the grandparents being escorted by the ushers, followed by the groom's aunt and uncle standing in for the groom's parents. Next, the mother of the bride was escorted by the ushers. Charlie's mother held her head high, exuding confidence as she made her way down the aisle. Her eyes shimmered with a mixture of pride and joy. Her indigo dress seemed to weave a tale of sophistication and strength. The guests whispered in awe as Charlie's mother took her seat.

The time had come for the groom to make his entrance. Bikori, standing tall at 6 feet one, exuded a magnetic presence. His mocha-colored skin seemed to glow under the warm lighting of the venue. With each step, he exuded confidence, his broad shoulders conveying strength and assurance. His short, well-groomed fade accentuated his sharp features, drawing attention to his striking appearance. As Bikori made his way down the aisle, his pearly whites gleamed, complementing his smile. The guests couldn't help but be enamored by Bikori's presence.

The music swelled, signaling the much-anticipated moment of the groomsmen and bridesmaids making their way down the aisle. The guests turned their attention to the entrance. The bridesmaids, dressed in flowing indigo blue gown, glided down the aisle with grace and unity. The shared dresses accentuated their figures, hugging them in all the right places. Their hair was meticulously styled in a bun twisted to the side, with ivory flowers adding an element of whimsy to their elegant ensembles.

Walking alongside the bridesmaids, the groomsmen stood tall and confident in black tuxedos. Their hair was impeccably styled, adding a touch of refinement to their overall appearance. Billie gasped for air as she saw Frankie, her breath taken away. "OMG! She's here!" she said to herself.

As the best man and the maid of honor reached the end of the aisle, their presence radiated with confidence. The crowd transformed into resounding applause, acknowledging their distinctive roles in the wedding party and their contribution to the overall tapestry of love and unity.

As the ring bearer and his mother reached the end of the aisle, the entire crowd erupted into applause, their hearts touched by the enduring display— the little boy wiping away his tears with the back of his hand. The guests eagerly awaited the appearance of the flower girl, little Bella, Charlie's cousin.

As Bella stepped onto the aisle, the crowd fell silent, their eyes fixed upon her. She was dressed in a delicate indigo-blue gown adorned with intricate white lace around the waist. Her golden locks were elegantly styled into a charming updo, adorned with ivory flowers that matched the floral theme of the wedding.

The moment had arrived. Charlie stood in the foyer with her dad, Mr. Morrison, waiting for the cue to come down the aisle. Charlie could sense that her father was nervous. "Daddy, are you okay?" she asked with a smile.

"Yeah, baby," her father replied. "The last time I came down the aisle was when I married your mother. Just a few butterflies, that's all. Don't worry, Daddy, I got you," Charlie said, blushing.

As the soft notes of the piano filled the air, Pastor Honeycutt's voice resonated throughout the crowded venue. His warm and soothing tone commanded attention, and everyone fell into a hushed silence.

"Ladies and gentlemen, family and friends, we gather here today to witness a truly remarkable moment," Pastor Honeycutt began, his eyes twinkling with anticipation. "Today, we celebrate the union of two souls, bound together by a love that knows no bounds. Please stand on your feet and welcome our radiant bride, Charlie, as she walks down the aisle."

The crowd stood up in unison, their eyes fixed on the entrance at the far end of the aisle. All eyes focused on the beautiful wooden doors, waiting for them to open and reveal Charlie's grand entrance. With a gentle creak, the doors swung open, and a collective gasp swept through the room.

Charlie, standing at 5 feet 11 inches tall, with her golden-brown skin glowing, took her first step into the sanctuary. Her long auburn hair cascaded down the middle, framing her radiant face. Dressed in an exquisite iris wedding gown, Charlie was a vision of elegance and charm. The gown trailed behind her, the train extending an impressive 10 feet, adding an air of regality to her presence. Walking beside her was her father, also resplendent in his tailored black tuxedo. His strong presence and supportive demeanor were a comforting anchor for Charlie. As they made their way down the aisle together, the love and pride between father and daughter were evident to all.

Pastor Honeycutt looked down at the wedding party and asked, "Who gives this bride away?" Standing in place and staring at his daughter with a smile, Mr. Morrison replied, "I do."

Pastor Honeycutt started the ceremony by saying, "We are gathered here to celebrate the union of Bikori Lee and Charlene Morrison. We are all here to support this commitment of love and to share with Bikori and Charlene as they choose to spend their lives together. Love has brought you together, and today, in the presence of your cherished loved ones, you shall declare your own vows, sealing your bond of eternity."

Bikori, with a confident smile on his face, turned to Charlie. With a deep breath, he began, "Charlene, from the moment I first laid eyes on you, I knew that you were the missing piece of the puzzle. You have shown me a love so pure and unconditional. Today, I promise to be your rock."

Looking out at the guests in the sanctuary, Bikori continued, "You know, we all know the saying, 'A good man is hard to find,' and sometimes, so is a good woman. And I just thank God we found each other. I love you, Charlie."

Bikori leaned in and whispered in Charlene's ear. "Guess what?" he asked. "What?" Charlie replied, blushing.

Bikori replied, "You're about to be my wife, girl!"

As Bikori uttered these words, the wedding guests were all in awe, and they started clapping. Charlene added, "I promise to be the best wife I can be. Our love is the most important thing in my life. I never thought I was worth a love of this magnitude, but here we are. I love you so much, Kori."

Bikori took his handkerchief and wiped Charlene's eyes. Pastor Honeycutt looked at the two of them and said, "I now pronounce you husband and wife. You may kiss your bride, son."

Bikori let out a "Whooee" and lifted the veil on Charlie's face before proceeding to kiss her. "Ladies and gentlemen, please stand on your feet as I present to you Mr. and Mrs. Bikori A. Lee," Pastor Honeycutt announced.

As her heart overwhelmed with joy, Charlie looked out at her wedding guests and exclaimed, "I's married now!" She held her wedding ring finger up for all to see.

The guests cheered and clapped, showering the couple with flower petals and confetti. The bride and groom beamed with joy and happiness, their hearts full of joy. Before the toast to the bride and groom, Billie, Teddy, and Suni sat together at the wedding table, whispering to each other. Suni leaned over and whispered in Teddy's ear, "I can't believe she came. Shit, neither can I, but she looks good," Teddy replied.

Charlie and Bikori stood up to acknowledge and thank their guests for coming. The sound of clinking glasses filled the air as Charlie spoke to get everyone's attention. "Can I have your attention, please?" Charlie said. "My husband and I would like to thank all of you guys for sharing this special day with us. Your presence at our wedding has added so much love to our special day."

"And last but not least, I would also like to give a shout-out to our wedding planner, Mille. Girl, you did your thang! Thank you for making our dreams come true." Charlie looked around and raised her glass, thanking

Mille, and the guests applauded. Mille responded with a smile, lifting her glass and bowing her head.

"And now, let's party," Charlie said as the DJ started playing.

At the reception, the DJ lowered the volume of the music to make an announcement. "At this time, we're going to have the bride and groom come to the center of the stage for the first dance." Charlie and Bikori made their way to the stage, surrounded by dimmed yellow lights. Charlie was in awe as the two embraced each other on the dance floor. The music began to play, and all eyes turned to the newlyweds as they took their first dance as husband and wife.

Charlie's flowing white gown swirled around her as Bikori took her hand and pulled her in close. The couple moved gracefully and effortlessly around the floor, twirling and dipping with ease. Their movements were synchronized as if they were one person. They looked deeply into each other's eyes, their love evident in the way they moved and the expressions on their faces.

Charlie told Bikori, "This is the happiest day of my life." Bikori replied with a smile, "I know, right! Don't get it twisted, Mrs. Lee, this is the happiest day of my life too." Charlie then mentioned, "You know, there is only one other thing that would make this day perfect." Bikori looked curious and asked, "What's that?" Charlie responded, with a flicker of gloom, "Having your parents here with us would have been the icing on the cake!" Bikori became a little emotional thinking about his parents. "Yes, sweetheart, you're absolutely right," he replied.

Charlie exclaimed, "Oh, baby, this feels like a dream." Bikori agreed, "Yeah, I know what you mean." They continued dancing to one of Charlie's favorite songs by Tony Terry. Charlie glanced over at Mille, who was leaning against the wall, sipping her champagne and watching them dance. Charlie said to Bikori, "Good call on Mille, babe. She was the perfect wedding planner." Bikori replied, "Yeah, that's how she paid her way through medical school." Charlie hummed and said, "She's hot, babe! I'm surprised you didn't snatch her up for yourself," blushing. They both looked over at Mille. Bikori responded, "Naw... She ain't my type." Charlie replied, "Yeah, right!" Bikori added, "Oh no, there you go!" They burst into laughter, looking into each other's eyes.

The wedding guests applauded as the first dance came to an end. They were mesmerized by the grace and beauty of the moment. The DJ, Mix

Master McQuay, called out, his voice carrying through the room, "That was quite the dance, ladies and gentlemen! Give it up for the bride and groom!" The crowd cheered loudly and energetically as Bikori and Charlie took their bow. As they began to walk off the stage, he said, "Hold up, Charlie. It seems like your girls have a request for tonight."

"They want to take a trip down memory lane, back in the day when you all used to perform in the talent shows together," the DJ, who was a classmate of theirs, looked out at the crowd and said. "Y'all remember when they used to put on those talent shows, dressing up like all the boy bands: New Edition, Silk, H-Town, High Five, Backstreet Boys, and *NSYNC!" The crowd responded by cheering and stomping their feet.

Billie, standing at 5 feet 3 inches tall, light-skinned, with high cheekbones, dreads, and China-doll eyes, stood up and started jumping up and down. "Yesssz... let's do this!" she yelled. All the ladies took center stage, with Charlie holding the microphone. "Are you guys ready?" she asked. The crowd went wild. Charlie looked over at Frankie with a smile. "Frankie, that means you too." Frankie blushed and shook her head, but the crowd urged her on. Frankie looked back at Travis for approval, and as he rubbed her back, he said, "Go ahead, baby, go do your thang!" Frankie took a deep breath, stood up, and joined the rest of the girls at center stage, where they began to dance and lip-sync to one of their favorite songs, "If It Isn't Love" by New Edition. Everybody was on their feet, clapping and rejoicing. Charlie was happy, and she looked over at Frankie and said, "This feels like old times, huh?" Frankie replied, "Yeah, something like that."

Charlie was having the time of her life. She was laughing and chatting with her friends and family, and her smile was contagious. While Bikori was chuckling with his boys, she continued to work the room, thanking and hugging as many guests as she could. Charlie spotted her Aunt Laura and walked toward her. "Aunt Laura, well, look at you! You're the most beautiful bride I've ever seen!" Aunt Laura exclaimed. "Thank you, Aunt Laura," Charlie replied.

Out of nowhere, Charlie became very emotional, and her Aunt Laura could see that something was wrong. "Aunt Laura, what is it? Are you alright?" Aunt Laura asked, hugging her tightly. She asked again, "What has you so upset?" She looked into Charlie's eyes and said, "Today is your wedding day. You're supposed to be happy, sweetie." Charlie replied, "You're right, TeTe. This is the happiest day of my life, but I find myself asking God, 'Why me?' It's almost like being rewarded for bad behavior. Do I really deserve this much happiness?" Aunt Laura tried to convince her to accept the joy that God had showered upon her. "You have to let it go, Charlie, and forgive yourself for what happened because God has," she said, grabbing Charlie's hands. "Look at me, you are a beautiful young woman with a good heart, and that is what matters. You have made some great choices in your life, and we're all very proud of you. Your Papa would be too if he were here."

As Charlie and Aunt Laura continued embracing each other, they were interrupted by Aunt Laura's daughter, Bella. She pulled on her mother's dress and said, "Mommy, I'm tired. I want to go home." "Okay, baby, I'm saying goodbye to your cousin Charlie, and then we will leave," Aunt Laura replied. Charlie stared at Bella with a huge smile on her face.

"Hey, Bella," Charlie said. "Aunt Laura, Bella was the prettiest flower girl I've ever seen!" Charlie exclaimed. "Well, we Morrison girls are known for our beauty," Aunt Laura replied proudly. Charlie nodded and said, "I know that's right!"

Aunt Laura looked at Charlie and said, "Listen, we're going to get out of here. Bella has practiced in the morning, and remember, whenever you're ready, I'm here for you. I love you so much, Aunt Laura." Charlie thanked her and replied, "Thank you again for everything."

Charlie waved to her little cousin and said, "Bye, Bella, take care." Bella replied, "Bye, Cousin Charlie!

Travis and Frankie start to mingle, working the room. "Hey Tyreke," Travis said as he extended his hand to Tyreke. "Hey, well, if it isn't Travis Richard Lawson the third, better known as RIPP! What's up, man?" Tyreke replied, shaking Travis's hand. "Nothing much. We're just living our best life," he said, glancing back at Marley. "Fancy, you're looking good as always," Tyreke complimented.

"Hey, Fancy, it's good to see you," Marley said. "You too, girl," Frankie replied. "Well, man, we're going to continue working the room. We want to hit the road before it gets too late. Nice seeing you, man!" Travis said.

Frankie grabbed Travis's hand and whispered, "Baby, look to your right. Look who's coming our way." "You got this, babe," Travis replied. Billie, Suni, and Teddy approached them. "Hey Travis and Frankie, long time no see," Billie greeted. "Hey, ladies! It's good to see you guys," Frankie responded. Smiling at Teddy, she added, "Girl, I see you're still rocking that short hair with that fire-red shade!" "Man, if I had a dollar for every time someone has said that to me...I... I'd be..."

Before Teddy could continue, Suni interrupted, standing at 5 feet 8 inches tall with slim mocha-colored skin, long black hair, and glasses. She said with a sarcastic look, "You would still be one broke bitch! As much as you be shopping." Teddy and the others chuckled. "Hey, girl, what's up?" Frankie greeted. "Hey Travis, I would like to introduce you guys to my fiancé, Blue!" Suni announced. Under her breath, Frankie muttered, "Damn!" Then she apologized, saying, "Oh, I'm sorry. It's very nice to meet you, Blue," Frankie replied, shaking Blue's hand. Travis chimed in, "Yeah, it's nice to meet you as well," as he shook Blue's hand.

Teddy said, "Frankie and Travis, I would like to introduce you to Cyd, my wife," Frankie mumbled under her breath, "What the fuck!" She quickly regained composure and said, "Oh, excuse my manners. It's nice to meet you, Cyd," Frankie greeted. Travis added, "Yeah, it's very nice to meet you, Cyd." Teddy concluded, "Guys, we're going to keep moving. It was very nice seeing you all again."

Frankie turned to Travis and said, "Hey, baby, I'll be right back. I'm going to find Charlie and say goodbye." Travis replied, "Sounds good, baby. And take your time. Let me find the groom and say goodbye."

As Frankie walked away to say goodbye to the bride, she couldn't help but look back at Teddy and mutter to herself, "Teddy is married to a woman? Ain't that about a bitch!" She approached Charlie, who greeted her warmly.

"Hey, Frankie! I'm glad to see you!" Charlie said with a smile.

Frankie replied, "Yeah, it's been a long time."

Charlie asked, "Is it okay to give you a hug?"

Frankie nodded and said, "Sure, why not." The two friends embraced, tears welling up in their eyes.

"I'm glad you accepted my invitation," Charlie said.

Frankie responded, "Yeah, I'm still not sure why I did, but here I am in front of you." As they chatted for a few minutes, it became evident that they had both grown and changed, and the bond they had shared in high school still lingered.

"Frankie, we were best friends a long time ago, and I really want that back," Charlie said, pouring out her heart.

Frankie looked at Charlie, her expression softening. "It's not just that. I miss how we used to be and the things we used to do."

Charlie pleaded, "Frankie, I promise you if given a second chance, you will see I'm different. And I want more than anything for us to be close again. I'll be back from my honeymoon in a couple of weeks. Will you be willing to join me for brunch at my house? There's so much I need to tell you."

Frankie nodded, understanding the depth of Charlie's emotions. "Sure, why not?" She glanced across the room at Travis, who was engrossed in conversation with Bikori and his friends.

"Hey, girl, I'm going to get my man before I have to meet somebody in the parking lot!" Frankie exclaimed.

Charlie chuckled and replied, "Yeah, please do! I always knew you and Travis would end up married. And he's still fine!"

Frankie agreed, "Yes, he is. I'll see you, girl." She slipped off her heels and walked away.

"Goodnight, see you soon," Charlie called after her. Frankie said her goodbyes to the rest of the girls and joined Travis at the door. They made their way to the car together.

Moments later, both Travis and Frankie were sitting in the car. Travis broke the silence. "Well... that was fun, huh?"

Frankie smiled and replied, "Yeah, I must admit, it wasn't too shabby." She had a peculiar look on her face, prompting Travis to ask, "Baby, what is it?"

Frankie exclaimed, "Babe! Teddy has a wife!"

Travis chuckled, saying, "Yeah, I didn't see that coming!"

Frankie added, "She reminds me of Cleo's boo from 'Set It Off' with the short blonde hair."

"Suni's fiancé, Blue, seems nice. I always knew she would end up with a white man," Frankie commented.

Travis chimed in, "Well, none of the brothers in high school ever showed any love!"

Frankie nodded in agreement, saying, "I know..."

Travis added, "And besides, love has no color!"

Frankie replied, "Yes, for sure!"

Travis turned to Frankie with a smile and asked, "You ready to hit the road, baby?"

Frankie responded enthusiastically, "Yes, let's do this!"

Travis smiled at Frankie and said, "Alright then, buckle up buttercup!" They took off in the car.

Back at the Majestic Hall, where the reception was taking place, everything was starting to wind down. Charlie and Bikori continued to thank their guests as they exited the building. Charlie's parents approached them.

"Baby girl, this was an event to remember. I love you, honey," Mr. Morrison said. "Bikori, take care of my baby girl. She's precious."

"I will, and thank you, sir. I'm honored to be a part of the family," Bikori replied.

As they said their final goodbyes, Charlie's parents hugged her once more, tears in their eyes. "We love you, sweetheart," her mother whispered, holding her close.

"I love you guys, too," Charlie replied.

Teddy and Cyd approached Charlie and Bikori to say their goodbyes.

"Hey, sister friend! This was definitely an event to remember, and I was here for it, sis!" Teddy exclaimed.

"Thank you, sis!" Charlie replied.

Teddy and Cyd headed for the door. They left the wedding reception, got in the car, and decided to take a shortcut through a dark road called Love Joy Lane, thinking it would be quicker to get to the main highway.

"That was a beautiful wedding," Cyd said, smiling at Teddy.

"Yeah, it was. It was almost as beautiful as ours," Teddy replied, winking at Cyd. "Pass me a cigarette, baby."

"Sure, baby. Would you like me to light it for you?" Cyd flirted, licking her lips.

"Oh, by all means, please do!" Teddy blushed.

As Cyd leaned in to light Teddy's cigarette, suddenly, Cyd screamed!

"Oh shit!" Teddy swerved into a ditch, hitting a tree to avoid hitting what appeared to be someone standing in the middle of the road.

Teddy hit her head on the dashboard, and the car spun into the dark woods. Teddy grabbed Cyd. "Baby, are you okay?"

"Yes, Teddy, I'm okay," Cyd said in a low tone.

Teddy looked in her rearview mirror and noticed someone in a black hoodie standing in the middle of the road. "What the fuck!" she exclaimed, screeching her eyes.

Teddy yelled out the window, "What the fuck, man! Are you crazy?" Because it was dark and foggy that night, Teddy wasn't able to see the person's face. She decided to get out of the car and approach the person, but they had already run away, leaving behind a burning newspaper clipping and a picture of a familiar face with a note attached that stated, "THIS IS ONLY THE BEGINNING!"

Teddy was shaken by the picture. She grabbed it and walked back to the car, her heart pounding.

Cyd asked anxiously, "What is it, baby? Did you see anything?"

Teddy, breathing heavily, replied, "No, baby, not really. It was too dark."
Cyd noticed something in Teddy's hand and asked, "What's in your hand, bae?"

Teddy shook her head and said, "Nothing important. Let's go home," her hands trembling.

CHAPTER 3

Two weeks had passed since Frankie and Charlie last spoke. Frankie stood on Charlie's doorstep, dressed casually in a vibrant yellow summer dress and sandals. Her mind was flooded with reservations as she contemplated their reunion after a decade of silence. As she stood there, she could already smell the aroma of freshly brewed coffee and the tantalizing scent of bacon wafting through the air. Her stomach rumbled in anticipation.

"If nothing else good comes from this reunion, at least I'm getting a decent meal out of it. That girl always knew how to cook. She got that from her grandmother," Frankie thought, licking her lips.

Taking a deep breath, Frankie was determined to push past her hesitation. She raised her hand and gently knocked on the sturdy wooden door. Charlie promptly answered, her face lighting up with a radiant smile.

"Hey, girl. You made it!" Charlie exclaimed, embracing Frankie in a warm hug.

Charlie led Frankie towards the cozy kitchen, where a beautifully set table awaited them. Sunlight streamed through the window, casting a warm glow on the flowers adorning the centerpiece. Plates piled high with fluffy pancakes, a platter of potatoes, and an assortment of fresh fruit caught Frankie's delighted gaze.

"Damn girl! Are you expecting anybody else?" Frankie asked, looking a bit confused.

"No, why do you ask?" Charlie replied, puzzled.

"Look at all this food. Who do you think is going to eat all this?" Frankie chuckled.

"I just wanted to make sure I had everything covered," Charlie explained.

"Come on in, have a seat, and dig in," Charlie invited.

"Thanks, girl. Lovely home," Frankie complimented, glancing around the inviting space.

"Thank you. As you can see, we have bacon, eggs, quiche, pancakes, and smothered potatoes. Take your pick. I'm just gonna have me some cold chicken and greens from last night's dinner, and you're welcome to that as well," Charlie chuckled.

Frankie marveled at Charlie's culinary skills. "Charlie, you've really outdone yourself this time. It all looks incredible, well... except for..."

"Except for what?" Charlie inquired, curious.

"That nasty-looking pickled jar. I remember when I used to go with you to your grandma's house, she always kept that pickled jar full of vinegar and peppers for her greens and cornbread. I see you're continuing the tradition!" Frankie grimaced.

"Girl, I don't know what you're talking about. Shoot, this is good!" Charlie laughed.

"To each their own, lady," Frankie smiled and laughed. "Shit, it's probably that same nasty-ass jar from 10 years ago!"

"Forget you, girl," Charlie playfully responded.

"I don't know, girl. This is starting to feel like old times," Charlie said with a nostalgic smile.

"Yeah, kind of," Frankie agreed, sharing the sentiment.

Charlie let out a sigh. "Girl, I've done a lot of soul-searching and growing up these last few years. I'm a changed woman, Frankie!"

Frankie nodded, acknowledging the impact Charlie's husband had on her.

"I guess your husband had a lot to do with that."

"Yes, somewhat," Charlie replied, shaking her head. "You know, I started writing you several letters over the years, but I didn't have the heart to follow through on any of them. But now I've missed you and our friendship so much," she said, wiping tears from her face. "Can you ever forgive me?"

Frankie reached out and held Charlie's hands. "I'm here, aren't I? Why are you crying, Charlie? What is it? You can tell me."

Charlie took a deep breath, preparing to speak her truth, but before she could, a loud knock interrupted their conversation.

"Excuse me, Frankie, while I get the door," Charlie said, walking towards it and scratching her head. The knocks became louder and louder, filling the air with anticipation.

Teddy and Charlie stand at the entrance of Charlie's home, engaging in conversation.

"Hey, girl," Teddy greets.

"Hey, sis, come on in," Charlie welcomes her.

Teddy looks around and notices someone else in the room.

"Oh, I didn't know you had company!" Teddy exclaims.

Charlie reassures her, "It's cool, girl. Come on in here."

As Teddy steps into the foyer, she expresses the need to talk.

"We need to talk," Teddy says, her voice filled with urgency.

Frankie, who had been standing nearby, offered to give them some privacy.

"Hey, I will give you guys some privacy," Frankie volunteers.

Teddy insists that Frankie should stay, as what she has to say involves all of them.

"No, you don't have to do that. I believe this involves you too," Teddy states, rubbing her head.

Charlie ponders whether they should call the other girls over.

"Should I have the other girls come over?" Charlie suggests.

Teddy agrees, "Yes, most definitely."

Later, all five girls gather on the patio of Charlie's house, ready for the important conversation.

"Okay, girl, we're all here now. Tell us what's going on!" Charlie requests.

Suni, intrigued and concerned, adds, "Yeah, girl, what's so important that I had to close the shop and come here? Girl, you are scaring me. What is it? Just spit it out!"

Teddy takes a deep breath and begins to explain the situation. "Okay, Cyd and I were leaving the reception, right? We decided to take the back road. As we were coming down Joy Lane, out of nowhere, someone appeared in the middle of the damn road. Before we knew it, we slid into the ditch to avoid hitting this person."

Charlie, eager for details, asks, "Did you get a look at that person?"

Teddy shakes her head, disappointment evident on her face. "No, all I saw in the rearview mirror was someone standing in the middle of the road, wearing jeans and a hoodie. I couldn't see the face! By the time I got out of the car to confront him, he was gone!"

Suni, puzzled, questions Teddy's statement. "Gone? What do you mean gone?"

Teddy shrugs, still trying to process what happened. "Hell, I don't know. He vanished into the woods, but he did manage to leave this behind!"

Teddy places a picture on the table, accompanied by a note. The group looks at the picture and notes in shock and disbelief.

Suni, curious about its origin, inquires, "Where did you get this?"

Teddy responds with frustration, "I just told you he left this in the middle

29

of the road! Weren't you listening?"

Trying to maintain calm, Suni reassures Teddy, "Okay, girl, just calm down."

Billie, visibly shaken, chimes in, "What do you think it means?"

Frankie picks up the picture, examines it closely, and asks a pointed question, "Who would do this?"

Teddy, smoking a cigarette, expresses her frustration and desire to move on from the past. "Hell, if I know. I've put this day behind me. I don't need this shit resurfacing again. This is my past, Cyd doesn't know anything about this, and I plan on keeping it that way."

The girls continue their conversation, discussing any unusual occurrences that have happened to them recently.

"Has anything out of the norm happened to anyone else?" Billie asks, nervously biting her fingernails.

Teddy turns to Suni, inquiring, "What about you, Suni? Anything strange?"

Suni contemplates for a moment before responding, "Now that you mention it, someone slashed my tires in front of the house last week!"

Teddy reacts with disbelief, rolling her eyes and shaking her head. "Okay, and you didn't think that was weird?"

Suni shrugs nonchalantly, "Hell, I didn't know. I just thought it was Blues' baby mama. You know she's been really salty since our engagement!"

Billie turns to Frankie, curious to hear her experience. "Anything out of the norm for you, Frankie?"

Frankie shakes her head, looking shocked. "No, I can't say that it has."

Teddy interjects, clapping her hands together. "Oh snap! That's right because Saint Frankie never does anything wrong!"

Frankie defends herself, raising her voice slightly. "I wouldn't call myself a saint, but I didn't have shit to do with any of that mess. That's on all of you."

Teddy responds, holding her cigarette, "Frankie, please don't try to come for me! Charlie is the one that had it out for her! Why that is, I don't know. Hell, I was just rolling with my girl!"

Frankie expresses her frustration, addressing the group. "I said over and over; leave her alone. But all of you continued to torment her for nothing until she couldn't take it anymore."

Concerned, Frankie turns to Charlie. "Charlie, you okay? I mean, you haven't said two words since we've been out here."

Charlie sits there in a daze, her emotions overwhelming her as tears stream down her face. Flashbacks haunt her, and the weight of guilt hangs heavy on her heart.

Teddy, frustrated with Charlie's silence, urges her, "Damn, Charlie, say something, anything, shit!"

Teddy's frustration continues, "Listen, don't get me wrong. We are responsible for this, but we have paid our dues. First, by getting expelled from school and not being able to walk across the stage with our classmates. It was really fucked up, and hell no, I won't be reliving this shit. I promise you!"

Billie interrupts, trying to calm the tension. "Yo, let's just all calm down! Let's face it, our attitudes were fucked up in high school. We were known as the mean girls back then. So let's just own that shit because once you know better, you do better, right? Let's just figure out a way to get through whatever this is together, alright?"

The group agrees, acknowledging the need for unity. Billie takes her leave, heading off to the practice, while Teddy also prepares to leave and pick up Cyd.

As Teddy attempts to open her car door, she hears a faint voice calling her name in the distance. Curiosity piqued, Teddy pauses and turns her attention toward the source of the voice, Frankie.

"Teddy!" Frankie shouts from the top of the hill in Charlie's backyard.

Teddy, taken aback by the sudden commotion, looks up at Frankie with a questioning expression. "What's up?" she asks.

Frankie stands at the top of the hill, a mischievous sparkle in her eyes. With a smirk on her face, she delivers a sarcastic message.

"Tell Cyd it was a pleasure meeting her," Frankie says, her voice dripping with sarcasm.

Teddy, a mixture of confusion and annoyance, mutters under her breath, "Yeah, whatever, bitch," as she drives off. Frankie watches her leave and remarks, "Damn hypocrite."

Charlie remains silent throughout the exchange, the weight of her past actions heavy on her shoulders.

CHAPTER 4

Billie sat at the practice this evening, a day she usually took off because one of her clients was getting married for the fourth time and wanted to be extra beautiful for her special day. Billie made an exception, working late to accommodate her client's request.

"Damn, Ms. Clair, I can't even get one husband, and here you are on number four!" Billie exclaimed, a hint of frustration evident in her voice.

Ms. Clair chuckled, aware of Billie's own romantic struggles. "Well, some people just have better luck, I suppose," she replied with a playful wink.

Billie warned, "Now, don't go touching your face. You remember what happened last time!" She pointed at Ms. Clair, recalling a humorous incident involving her previous Botox session.

Miss Clair burst into laughter, reminiscing about the mishap. "Oh, believe me, Billie, I've learned my lesson," she said, her eyes twinkling with amusement. "I won't be making that mistake again."

Billie stood up from her chair, wearing a mischievous grin. "You sit tight. I'm going to get you some warm tea," she said, rubbing her shoulders. Miss Clair nodded gratefully, appreciating the kind gesture. "Thank you, Billie. That sounds lovely. I could use a pick-me-up."

Humming her favorite song by HER, Billie made her way to the break room to prepare some tea for Ms. Clair. As she reached for the tea canister on the countertop, a sudden power outage plunged the room into darkness. The overhead lights flickered off, leaving them momentarily confused.

"Oh, shit!" Billie exclaimed, her voice filled with surprise. In the darkness, her grip on the glass loosened, and it slipped from her hand, shattering as it hit the floor. Billie fumbled in her pocket for her phone and activated the flashlight. Its dim glow illuminated the shattered glass scattered across the floor.

"Is everything okay?" Miss Clair shouted from the other room.

"Stay where you are, Miss Clair. I'm going to fix the lights," Billie yelled down the hall. "As soon as I can find the damn circuit breaker," she mumbled under her breath.

Miss Clair's voice filled with genuine care as she said, "Be careful, Billie. We don't want you getting hurt."

Billie smiled warmly, appreciating Miss Clair's concern. "Don't worry, I've got it under control," she reassured her with a steady voice.

Billie held the light up on her phone as she walked down the hall, searching for the circuit breaker while trying to fight off panic. Eventually, she found it, and with a flick of a switch, the lights came back on. She let out a relieved sigh, thanking her lucky stars.

"Thank God," Miss Clair exclaimed with a sigh of relief.

"Okay, Miss Clair, let's get you out of here. You have a big day tomorrow," Billie said, smiling at her. She gave Miss Clair a hug and closed the door behind her.

Billie proceeded to the spa room, where she had performed Botox on Miss Clair earlier. She sighed, wiping her forehead. "Another day, another fifty cents," she muttered, looking at the tip in her hand. "Oh well, let me clean this stuff up so I can get out of here."

Just as Billie was finishing up, the doorbell rang through the practice.
"Who could that be?" Billie wondered aloud, looking startled and curious. She stopped what she was doing and headed towards the main door of the practice.

"Ms. Clair, is that you? What did you forget?" Billie asked, smiling and shaking her head as she walked to the door.

Billie opened the door only to find no one there. "Hello, anybody out there?" she called out, looking left and right. With no response, she stepped back inside, closing the door behind her. "Guess I'm done."

Billie locked up the practice, grabbed her purse and keys, and headed to her car. As she walked through the dark night, she couldn't shake the feeling of being followed. Every time she turned around, there was no one there.

"Man, it's dark out here," she mumbled to herself. Taking out her keys, she unlocked the doors to her car, and just as she closed the door behind her, her phone started ringing.

"Hello?" Billie answered, still a bit on edge.

"Hey girl, what's up?" came the voice on the other end of the line.

Billie smiled, recognizing her friend's voice. "Girl, just leaving the practice," she replied, putting on lipstick as she drove. "What's up with you?"

"I was going to see if you wanted to meet me over at the Happy Hour Bar and Grill to watch this NBA game?" her friend suggested.

"No, boo boo, sister girl got a date tonight," Billie said, smiling. "I hope I can keep my eyes open. Ms. Clair wore me out!" she chuckled, shaking her head.

"I hear that. Who is this scrub?" her friend inquired, a hint of concern in her voice.

"Awe damn, here we go!" Billie laughed. "He's somebody I met online."

"Be careful, sis. You still have that tracker on your phone?" her friend reminded her.

"Yeah, I do," Billie reassured her.

The conversation shifted, and her friend asked, "But what do you think about the stuff that went down today at Charlie's house? It really has me freaked out!"

"Girl, me too! Who do you think is behind this?" Billie asked, her voice filled with concern.

"I wish I knew! This is scary," her friend replied.

"I know, but try not to panic yet," Billie advised. "Go have a drink with your beautiful wife. You better not be too late because you have work in the morning!"

"Who gon check me!" her friend playfully responded. "Yeah, being your own boss has its perks."

"Alright, I'll see you at work tomorrow. Okay?" Billie said.

Billie hung up the phone, turned up the volume on her radio, and began singing as she continued driving to meet her date. But suddenly, her car's engine sputtered and backfired, indicating it was about to run out of gas. Eventually, the car came to a complete stop.

"Oh no," Billie sighed, her frustration evident. Turning the key and pressing her foot on the accelerator one last time, she muttered, "I know I didn't just run out of gas!"

As she closed her eyes for a second, feeling a wave of exhaustion, a shiver ran down her spine, causing her to jolt upright. She noticed a figure in her rearview mirror—an ominous silhouette draped in a mass and black hoodie. Panic gripped her as she reached for her phone, but before she could react, the figure lunged from the back seat and clamped a gloved hand over her mouth, suffocating her scream.

Billie's eyes widened in terror, her body tensing as she desperately fought against the intruder's hold. She thrashed and kicked, trying to escape, but the grip remained unyielding. The unknown person leaned into her, their gloved hands stifling any sound she could make.

A mouth was shushing her constantly as she continued to kick and scream in defense until she took her last breath and was then drugged from her car. At 2 A.M., Charlie lay in bed next to her husband, her mind consumed by a haunting nightmare. "No, no, I'm sorry!" she screamed, her voice echoing through the room. Tossing and turning, she relived the horrifying image of Brandy lying on the ground. Bikori, her husband, woke up, shaking her gently. "Baby, baby," he called softly, trying to bring her back to reality. "You're having a nightmare."

He held her tightly, comforting her as she gasped for air, her body trembling with fear. Beads of perspiration glistened on her forehead, and her heart raced in her chest. Charlie sat up in bed, still catching her breath.

"Baby, it's okay," Bikori reassured her, his voice filled with love and concern. "You were just having a nightmare. I've got you, babe."

"You've been having a lot of nightmares, babe," Bikori stated, sitting beside her. "What's wrong? Please tell me! Whatever it is, you can tell me. I'm here for you. I got you!"

Charlie sat in bed, her eyes closed, contemplating whether to reveal a secret from her past to Bikori, her husband. Fear gripped her heart as she considered the potential consequences. She took a deep breath, holding Bikori's hands tightly.

"There's something about my past I need to share with you, but I'm afraid," Charlie finally confessed, her voice quivering.

Bikori squeezed her hand reassuringly, reminding her of their commitment to each other. "This is a no-judgment zone, babe," he assured her, his eyes filled with love. "For better or worse, remember? You can tell me anything. I'm here for you."

Encouraged by his unwavering support, Charlie closed her eyes, gathering her thoughts before she began her revelation. Just as she was about to speak, the sound of a pager interrupted the moment, breaking their connection.

"Beep! Beep! Beep!" the pager resounded, demanding Bikori's attention.

"Oh, shit! Babe, that's the hospital," Bikori exclaimed, his voice filled with urgency. "I've got to go."

Disappointment flickered in Charlie's eyes, but she nodded, understanding the importance of Bikori's work. "We'll finish this conversation later, okay? It's going to be okay," he reassured her, accepting the kiss he planted on her forehead. Bikori hurriedly dressed himself, leaving Charlie alone with her thoughts.

She lay in bed, clutching her pillow tightly, her mind consumed by the weight of unspoken words and unresolved secrets. The room felt silent and heavy as she contemplated the right time and place to share her past with Bikori.

Charlie sat in her office at Brown Sugar Incorporated, going through the mail as she waited for her first client. Glancing outside her window, she noticed a lengthy line forming outside Billie's office.

"Where is Billie?" Charlie wondered aloud, chuckling to herself as she observed the crowd. "Got these people out here lined up at her door like they're waiting for government cheese."

Curiosity got the best of her, and Charlie decided to call Billie on the phone. After several rings, it went to voicemail.

"Hello, what up, girl?" Charlie greeted with a smile. "Just checking on you because you've got money lined up outside your door. And you know our motto: If it doesn't make money, it doesn't make sense! Hopefully, you're on your way, girl. I'll see you when you get here."

Feeling a sense of unease, Charlie raised her hands in the air, trying to catch Teddy's attention from her adjacent sports rehabilitation office. Teddy noticed her and approached the window.

"Ring, ring!" Charlie called out, putting her phone up to her ear.
Teddy picked up the call. "Hey, what's up?"

"Hey, Teddy," Charlie began. "I was just wondering if you've talked to Billie today?"

"Not since last night. Why?" Teddy replied, curiosity in his voice.

"I tried calling her, but she didn't answer. There were people out there waiting on her," Charlie explained, a hint of concern in her tone.

"Well, ain't nobody out there now," Teddy said, peering out the window. "Seems like she finally dragged her butt out of bed," she added, chuckling.

Changing the subject, Charlie asked, "Have you seen Suni yet?"

"Yeah, she's here," Teddy replied. "But she told me she's leaving early today because she and Blue are going to look at some venues."

Charlie nodded, a smile forming on her face. "I heard that. Alright, girl, I'll talk to you later."

Later that evening, as the day ended, Charlie went to Billie's office, hoping to catch up with her before she left. She opened the door, expecting to find her friend inside.

But to her surprise, the office was empty. Billie was nowhere to be seen. Concern etched on her face, Charlie wondered where Billie could be and why she hadn't shown up earlier.

Charlie's concern deepened as she scanned the office, searching for any sign of Billie's whereabouts. With a smile, she greeted one of Billie's staff nurses.

"Hey, where's your boss?" Charlie asked, trying to hide her growing worry. "Hello!"

The nurse, washing her hands with a nervous look on her face, responded, "I haven't seen her today. I mean, she didn't come in. I checked her calendar, and it was blank."

Charlie's heart raced, her breathing becoming heavier with each passing second. Something was definitely wrong. She reached for her phone and dialed Teddy's number, desperately seeking answers.

CHAPTER 5

The sun hung high in the sky as Charlie's house became a hub of anxiety and determination. The group, consisting of Charlie, Teddy, and Suni, gathered in the living room, their faces etched with worry and determination.

"Teddy, you have to tell the police about the night of the wedding!" Charlie urged; her voice laced with urgency.

Teddy's face contorted with frustration as she vehemently replied, "Oh hell no! We don't even know if these two incidents are related! Giving up that information means reliving our past, and that's not something I'm ready to do."

Suni interjected, her voice filled with compassion and determination. "I feel you, sis. I don't want to relive that shit either, but this is our sister we're talking about. We have to do whatever it takes!"

Teddy stood up, her resolve evident as she addressed the group. "Come on, y'all! How many women end up dead after online dating? We see that shit all the time on the news."

Suni's voice softened as she shared some information. "Well, that guy has been cooperative with the police department. He passed the polygraph test; so far, he's clean."

As they deliberated their next move, the doorbell rang, causing Charlie to jump up and rush to the door, hopeful for any news or lead.

"Doorbell rings," Charlie murmured to herself, her heart pounding in her chest. With anticipation, she swung open the door.

Frankie stood before her; her eyes filled with concern. "Hey, girl, I got here as quickly as I could," she said, her voice carrying a sense of urgency.

Teddy, standing nearby, crossed her arms and stared at Frankie, her expression guarded. "What the hell is she doing here?" Teddy blurted out; her frustration evident.

Frankie stepped closer to Teddy; her eyes unblinking. "Well, I'm not here for you, that's for damn sure."

Teddy, exasperated, threw her hands up in the air. "Poof, be gone shit," she replied, a mix of anger and resignation in her voice.

Suni, determined to bring the focus back to their missing friend, intervened, pointing her finger at both Teddy and Frankie. "This shit between you two must stop! Let's just squash it now and focus on finding Billie."

Teddy looked at Frankie, her gaze softened. "Listen, I'm sorry, okay? It's not even about you. I'm tired of this shit, man! We have paid for our mistakes. Hell, we're still paying for them."

Charlie, trying to diffuse the tension, shushed the group. "Hey, guys, the news is on," she announced, hoping for any information or breakthrough that could help in their search for Billie.

The room fell into a hushed silence as all eyes turned toward the television. The news anchor's voice filled the room, broadcasting updates and stories that seemed worlds away from their current predicament.

The reporter's voice echoed through the room, "The small town of Dogwood, with its quaint houses and tight-knit community, is buzzing with concern and unity." People gathered in the town square, their worried faces reflecting the gravity of the situation. A makeshift bulletin board was erected, adorned with pictures of a smiling Willow Stephenson, who went missing. Billie's car was found a mile away from Brown Sugar Incorporated. The Stephenson family firmly believed that foul play may be involved. Mark and Johnny, Billie's brothers, led the press conference.

Amidst the hushed murmurs and nervous shuffling, Mark's voice cut through the silence, filling the square with a mix of urgency and hope.

"Everyone, may I have your attention, please," Mark announced, commanding the crowd's focus. "Please, if you have any information about my sister, please come forward. Billie, we will find you."

Frankie abruptly stood up, her determination shining through. "I'm going to call Travis. Maybe he can contact Deuce. He works for the 7th district. Before we go public with everything, let's see if he can help us. He has connections."

All four women agreed, understanding the need for a strategic approach before revealing everything to the public. They knew that their friend's life was at stake, and they were willing to explore any avenue that could lead to her safe return.

As the front door swung open, Bikori, Charlie's husband, stepped inside, his eyes widening in surprise at the sight of the distressed group.

"Hey, baby," Bikori greeted Charlie with a kiss on the forehead. "Hey, ladies. Is everything okay?"

Charlie, overwhelmed by her emotions, broke down in tears, seeking solace in her husband's comforting embrace. "No, baby, it's not okay," she cried hysterically.

Bikori held Charlie close, offering comfort and reassurance. Teddy, recognizing the need for privacy, spoke up. "Come on, ladies. Let's give them some privacy."

The three women nodded in agreement and began walking toward the door, but Charlie stopped them.

"Ladies, it's time," Charlie declared, her voice filled with determination and pain. They all exchanged knowing glances, realizing that the moment they had been preparing for had arrived.

Looking at Bikori with swollen eyes, Charlie said, "Baby, it's time," her voice trembling with sadness.

"It's okay, baby, I've got you," Bikori reassured Charlie, his voice filled with love and determination.

The following day, inside the bustling 7th District Police Station, the officers found themselves engrossed in a lively discussion about the upcoming NBA Finals. As they debated the teams' chances, Deuce and his partners shared laughter and spirited banter, their voices filling the office.

"Man, now y'all know LeBron and the Lakers are going to win the NBA Finals! Clean sweep! Game 4," Deuce exclaimed, clapping and laughing. "Who wants to put some money on it?"

Amidst the friendly trash-talking, Deuce's phone rang, surprising him amidst the NBA chatter. Curious about the call's interruption, he quickly answered, momentarily shifting his focus away from the game predictions.

"Hello?" Deuce answered, his voice filled with surprise.

"Travis, what's up, playa!" Deuce greeted his friend.

"What's up, man! What's going on with you?" Deuce asked, a smile playing on his lips.

"I need your help with a situation. Can you help me?" Travis's voice sounded serious and concerned.

"No doubt! Help my boy, hell yeah!" Deuce replied confidently.

"It has something to do with girls," Travis revealed.

As Deuce hung up the phone, his mind raced with thoughts about the situation involving girls. "What did these girls get themselves into now?" he pondered, his expression filled with both curiosity and concern.

Later that evening, in the comfort of Charlie's bedroom, while Bikori enjoyed a shower, Charlie lay in bed, her eyes fixed on her handsome partner. The dimly lit room was interrupted by the glow of her vibrating cellphone, drawing her curiosity.

As she picked up the phone, a new group text message appeared on the screen, prompting her immediate attention. The message asked if everyone was okay and if important conversations had taken place that night. Charlie swiftly replied, sharing the newfound sense of freedom she felt after talking to Bikori.

"Yes, I had a conversation with my man. I feel so free now, and he said we are in this together," Charlie typed, her heart filled with relief and gratitude.

Teddy and the other ladies chimed in, expressing their own conversations and the support they received. The messages exchanged within the group carried a sense of unity and understanding.

"Everything is good over here," Suni responded, her message filled with reassurance.

Charlie proposed a plan for the next day. "Let's all touch base at work tomorrow and pray the police have made some progress."

With their agreement confirmed through text messages, the four women ended the conversation and hung up their phones.

In the early hours of the morning, as a storm raged outside, Charlie found herself awakened by the thunder, lightning, and heavy rain hitting her bedroom window. The intense weather captivated her attention, causing her to contemplate the power of nature's forces.

An hour later, still enveloped in the darkness, Charlie's sleep was once again disrupted by the relentless rain and dazzling lightning. She gazed up at the ceiling, illuminated by each burst of light, while beside her, Bikori peacefully slept, seemingly undisturbed by the storm's fury.

Amused by his ability to sleep soundly, Charlie rubbed his head, savoring the intimate moment shared in the midst of the storm.

Charlie lay in bed, feeling dazed and overwhelmed by the storm's intensity. Seeking respite from the bright light seeping through the window, she decided to cover her face with her pillow, hoping to find solace in the darkness.

Suddenly, a jarring sound echoed through the room, resembling the impact of large rocks against the windowpane. Startled, Charlie's heart raced as she uttered in disbelief, "Oh shit! Please tell me that's not hail!" The noise intensified, growing louder and more forceful with each passing moment.

Gathering her courage, Charlie mustered the determination to investigate the source of the commotion. She stole a glance at Bikori, cautiously attempting to slip out from under the covers without disturbing him. Tip-toeing towards the window, she peeked outside, ensuring everything was alright.

"Well, it didn't look like there was any damage. I guess it was just coming down hard," Charlie murmured, her gaze fixed on the torrential downpour. With a sigh, she closed the curtains, attempting to block out the unsettling sounds and sights.

Just as she began to head back toward the safety of her bed, something stopped her dead in her tracks. A surge of fear coursed through her veins, causing her body to tremble and her breaths to grow heavy. Slowly, she mustered the strength to turn around and face whatever awaited her.

With each step she took, her breathing became more labored, her anxiety reaching its peak. She mustered the courage to take one last breath before reopening the curtains, bracing herself for what she might find. However, to her immense relief, there was no one there. A sigh escaped her lips, releasing the tension that had gripped her.

Standing there with her eyes closed, she whispered to herself, "Girl, stop tripping! And take your butt to bed."

A loud noise erupted out of nowhere. Startled, Charlie's exclamation of "Fuck!" echoed through the room, her eyes snapping open. To her horror, a figure dressed in a black hoodie and mask stood ominously at the window. Fear coursed through her veins as she let out a piercing scream, collapsing to the floor in shock. The lightning illuminated the stranger's face, intensifying the terror of the moment.

Awakened by Charlie's horrific scream, Bikori sprang into action, rushing to her side as she lay on the floor. Gasping for air, Charlie pointed towards the window, her trembling finger indicating the intruder. Bikori's protective instincts kicked in as he ran to the window, only to catch a glimpse of the mysterious person fleeing down the street.

"Stay right here, baby. I'm going to check it out," Bikori reassured Charlie before darting out of the front door, braving the rain in pursuit of the intruder. However, his efforts proved futile as the person managed to elude him. He returned to the house, realizing that he had forgotten to turn off the alarm.

Running back inside, Bikori rushed to Charlie's side, embracing her tightly, determined to reassure her that they were safe. "Oh well, at least I don't have to call the cops," he remarked, attempting to lighten the mood amidst the tension, his arms wrapped protectively around her.

As they sat in the living room, a loud doorbell jarred them awake and alerted them. Detective Johnston and Detective Kent arrived at the scene, their presence announced by the ringing doorbell. Bikori, consoling Charlie, instructed her to wait as he went to answer the door. He kissed her forehead before rising from his seat and making his way to the entrance.

Opening the door, Bikori was momentarily blinded by the flashing police lights, shielding his eyes with his arms. Detective Johnston introduced himself, accompanied by Detective Kent, and requested permission to enter the house. Bikori obliged, welcoming them inside.

"Good evening, Mr. and Mrs. Lee, right?" Detective Johnston addressed them, seeking confirmation.

"That's Dr. Lee," Bikori corrected, emphasizing their professional titles.

Detective Johnston acknowledged the distinction with respect, then gestured for them to start from the beginning, inviting them to recount the events that had transpired. Bikori turned to Charlie, prompting her with care, "Baby, are you ready to tell them what happened?"

Bikori continued to console Charlie, who sat there in a daze, shaking her head, and wiping her tears. Detective Johnston reassured her to take her time, emphasizing that they were not in any hurry.

In the midst of the interview, one of the police officers collecting evidence outside the house interrupted them. The rookie police officer handed Detective Johnston three items that were found near the bedroom window. Among them was a picture of the starting five with the words "payback's a bitch" written on it, a news article clipping about Brandy Alexander, who had committed suicide, and a necklace engraved with the words "FAMILY FIRST."

As Charlie laid eyes on the necklace, she became hysterical, shaking and breathing heavily. Detective Johnston asked if any of it looked familiar to her. In a stoic state, Charlie nodded and admitted that the necklace was indeed familiar, triggering flashbacks of Brandy lying on the ground with the necklace around her neck, the words "FAMILY FIRST" imprinted on it.

Bikori, being there by Charlie's side, encouraged her not to be afraid to share her past with the detectives, assuring her that he was with her every step of the way. With his support, Charlie gathered her courage and prepared to speak.

Wrapping up the interview with Charlie and Bikori, Detective Johnston shook his head in understanding, urging Charlie to take her time as she began to share her story. The detectives thanked the couple for their cooperation and assured them that they would be in touch.

In the early morning hours, as dawn approached, Bikori sat on the edge of the bed, expressing how proud he was of Charlie. She looked at him and smiled, thanking him for his support and love.

CHAPTER 6

Bikori and Charlie pulled up in front of the Brown Sugar practice. Before letting Charlie out of the car, Bikori put the car in park and had a quick conversation with her.

"How are you feeling?" Bikori asked, looking at Charlie.

"I'm okay, my love, and you didn't have to drive me to work," Charlie replied, smiling at Bikori.

"It's my pleasure, my love. Hopefully, the police will be here this afternoon to follow you home, and the detective said we should know something in a couple of days about the fingerprints. It might take a little longer with everything going on with this new coronavirus. Hopefully, we'll get some answers before the governor starts shutting everything down," Bikori said, looking at her with hope.

"What in the HELL!" Bikori exclaimed suddenly.

"Yeah, I figured there would be news reporters out here today after my talk with the police last night," Charlie said.

"Hold up, babe, let me walk you in," Bikori said.

"Sure," Charlie agreed.

Bikori turned off the car and walked around to the passenger side to let Charlie out. He took her hand, and they walked towards the building, bypassing the reporters.

"Move, move, get out of our way," Bikori said, pushing through the crowd to get Charlie inside the building. "Have a good day, baby."

Charlie looked over at Billie's office door, which had a temporary closed sign on it. She closed her eyes and prayed to God to bring Billie home safely.

Inside Suni's Pharmacy, patients in the waiting area were intrigued by the top story on Channel 4 News.

"There continues to be an outpouring of love and support from the community for Willow Stephenson, who went missing over a week ago not far from this building, her place of employment, Brown Sugar the Practice," the reporter on the news announced. "You may remember Willow from years earlier; she was part of a group of girls known as the Staring 5 who bullied a transgender female named Brandy Alexander in high school. As a result, Brandy committed suicide."

Suni stood at the counter, trying to ignore the news. A customer approached her.

"Hi, can I help you?" Suni asked.

The customer looked behind the counter and asked, "Is Lisa, the pharmacy tech, still here?"

Suni replied slowly, "She is, but I can help you. Are you picking up? If so, what's your name?"

"Stacey Ellis," the customer replied, looking around nervously.

Suni smiled at the customer and said, "I'll be right back."

The customer rolled her eyes at Suni as she walked away from the counter.

"That will be $10.95," Suni said when she returned.

The customer handed her the money and looked at Suni with disgust. "You're one of them, aren't you?" she said, glancing at the TV and then back at Suni.

"I'm afraid so," Suni replied, looking at the news as she handed the customer the medicine.

The customer walked away, shaking her head. Suni stood there, tearing up, but she managed to pull herself together and carry on with her day.

The girls decided to meet up for drinks and to talk after work at the Happy Hour Bar and Grill. Charlie arrived and greeted Suni, Teddy, and Frankie with hugs.

"Hey, ladies," Charlie said, embracing them.

Frankie looked out the window and asked, "Charlie, did you just get dropped off by the police?"

"No, but he followed me here. Since what happened last night, Bikori got me 24-hour police protection until we hear back from the detectives," Charlie explained.

Frankie held Charlie's hand in support. Suni expressed her fear for their safety.

"I'm so afraid for us, y'all! The world looks at us again with hate. I'm a good person," Suni said, her voice trembling as she cried and sipped her wine. "I have changed. We all have. Who is this bastard? And what the hell does he want from us after all this time?"

Teddy shrugged in response, feeling just as uncertain. The girls sat together, contemplating the unknown, their thoughts swirling with fear and unanswered questions.

The weight of their shared secrets finally lifted, and the girls sat together at the Happy Hour Bar and Grill, expressing their relief and determination. Teddy, fueled by a newfound liberation, voiced her thoughts.

"Shit, we knew that was going to happen as soon as we aired out our dirty laundry! But you know what, I don't give a damn anymore. I feel so relieved this shit is out in the open. No more secrets, right Charlie?" Teddy exclaimed, her emotions running high.

All eyes turned to Charlie, who sat there in a daze, her mind filled with haunting images of Brandy lying on the ground, blood surrounding her.

Overwhelmed, Charlie burst into tears, unable to contain her emotions any longer. Frankie held her hands tightly, offering comfort and support.

"Hopefully, the police will catch whoever is behind this. I know I haven't been here for a long time, but I'm here now," Frankie assured Charlie, her voice filled with determination.

Teddy, looking into Charlie's eyes, expressed her concern. She emphasized the importance of uncovering any information that could lead them to the culprit.

"We got you, sis. If there's something that's going to help us catch this motherfucker, then we need to know," Teddy affirmed, her gaze unwavering.

Suni joined in, echoing the sentiment of support for Charlie. Together, they reassured her that they were there for her no matter what.

Charlie wiped her tears and made a promise to share what she had been holding onto for so long. However, she emphasized the need to address something important before revealing the truth.

As their conversation came to an end, they acknowledged the uncertainty of the times, with rising coronavirus cases and talks of a potential shutdown. They came together in prayer, holding hands and seeking solace from a higher power.

With closed eyes and bowed heads, they prayed for their missing friend Billie's safe return. They asked for strength for Billie's family and protection for all their sisters.

"Amen," they all said in unison, their voices filled with hope and determination.

Outside the Happy Hour Bar and Grill, the four ladies bid each other farewell. Frankie waved at the others and headed towards her car. Little did she know that her evening was about to take an unexpected turn.

Unlocking her car doors, Frankie noticed a black Jaguar with tinted windows parked nearby. She admired the car briefly before driving off, blasting her music.

As she continued her journey, she couldn't shake the feeling that the same car was tailing her. Growing suspicious, Frankie slowed down and eventually came to a complete stop. Glancing in her rearview mirror, she saw the black car stop as well.

Confused and on edge, Frankie cautiously accelerated, trying to put some distance between them. But the car persisted, remaining behind hers.

"What the hell?" Frankie exclaimed, her breath heavy with apprehension. She continued driving, becoming increasingly wary of the persistent car following her.

Eventually, Frankie made the decision to slow down once again, coming to a complete stop. Staring at the car behind her, she realized it had also come to a stop.

Feeling a surge of unease, Frankie cautiously stepped on the accelerator, gradually increasing her speed.

Frankie's heart raced as she was startled by the loud screeching sound of the pursuing car quickly overtaking hers. She let out a frustrated curse as·the car passed by, the burning rubber smell lingering in the air.

"What the hell was that all about? At least that car is gone. Damn, I hate driving down this road! I hope a deer doesn't appear," Frankie muttered to herself, trying to regain her composure.

She continued driving, finally reaching Spanish Trails, a long road that led to her subdivision. The familiar surroundings provided a sense of relief, and Frankie pressed on, eager to reach the safety of her destination.

At Brother's Dart Lounge, Travis and Deuce decided to meet up for drinks and catch up.

"Man, have you gotten any updates about the case?" Travis asked, taking a sip of his beer.

"Naw, man," Deuce replied, shaking his head. "With everything going on with this coronavirus, the Forensic Analysis Department is running just a little behind. Hopefully, when these fingerprints come back, it will tell us something."

Travis mentioned a promising new vaccine he had heard about on CNN and asked if Deuce planned to get it. Deuce scoffed at the idea.

"Shit! With that foolery we got going on in the White House right now, hell naw!" Deuce exclaimed, chuckling.

Travis chuckled in response. They shifted the conversation to Frankie's well-being and her worries about Billie.

"She's good, just worried about Billie," Travis informed Deuce.

Meanwhile, Frankie continued driving down Spanish Trails Road. Suddenly, out of nowhere, another car rear-ended hers with a loud bang!

Frankie let out a scream, her voice filled with terror. Her heart pounded against her chest as she stole a quick glance in the rearview mirror, confirming her worst fears. The headlights of the pursuing car bore down on her, growing larger and more menacing by the second. The car showed no signs of slowing down.

"FUCK!" Frankie cursed, her voice trembling. Desperately searching for a solution to escape her relentless pursuer, adrenaline surged through her veins. She made a quick decision and slammed her foot down on the accelerator, driving as fast as she could, determined to outrun the danger behind her.

Skrrrt! The car crashed into the back of Frankie's car, jolting her forward. She let out a scream of shock and frustration.

"Who the hell is this?" Frankie yelled, her voice filled with fear. The car behind her continued to repeatedly rear-end her vehicle, causing her to hit her head on the dashboard. In a panic, she screamed at her Bluetooth, "Call Travis! Call Travis!"

Desperate for help, Frankie tried to maintain control of her car while the relentless pursuer continued to trail her.

At Brother's Dart Lounge moments later, Travis's phone rang, and he looked down to see Frankie's call.

"Oh, here's my baby now!" Travis exclaimed with a smile. Deuce smirked, teasing him.

"Hey baby!" Travis answered, his voice filled with concern.

Frankie's voice trembled as she pleaded for help. "Baby, please help me! Someone is chasing me, and they won't slow down!"

Travis sprang out of his chair, ready to take action. "Hold on, baby. Slow down. Where are you?"

"He won't slow down, baby! Please help!" Frankie screamed, her desperation evident.

Travis quickly realized the urgency of the situation. "Bruh, we've got to go!" He motioned for Deuce to join him, and they headed out to find Frankie.

Frankie was still driving down Spanish Trails Road at high speed. She became more desperate with each passing moment. As she spotted the first house in sight, she made a split-second decision. It was pitch black, but she was focused. Determined to escape, she swerved her car onto the resident's grass, abruptly stopping her vehicle.

Frankie jumped out of the car, screaming for help. She ran up the steps to the neighbor's front door, her fist clenched. With each powerful knock, she pleaded, "Please help me! Please!"

The suspense grew as Frankie awaited a response, hoping that someone inside would come to her aid.

As Frankie looked back, she saw the car driving away, finally relieved that the relentless pursuer was gone. She turned her attention to the neighbor's house, hoping for safety and help.

The neighbor opened the door just as Frankie stumbled towards him, tears streaming down her face. Overwhelmed by fear and desperation, she cried out, "Please help me!"

The neighbor, taken aback by the distressing scene before him, tried to steady Frankie and offer comfort. He struggled to find the right words to console her.

"It's okay, it's okay," he reassured her, his voice filled with empathy. Sensing the urgency, he quickly opened the door, scanning the surroundings to ensure they were alone. In the distance, he spotted a car speeding away at the end of the subdivision. With a deep breath, he closed the door behind them, creating a sense of safety within the confines of his home.

Travis and Deuce, fueled by adrenaline and concern, swiftly arrived at the neighbor's house where Frankie had sought refuge. With screeching tires, they drove onto the neighbor's property, determined to reach Frankie as quickly as possible.

Travis jumped out of the car and ran towards Frankie, who was sitting on the porch, surrounded by flashing lights, as the police conducted their interview. Overwhelmed with relief, Frankie sobbed and embraced Travis tightly.

"Oh baby, I'm so glad you're here!" she cried, seeking solace in his arms.

Travis held her close, showering her forehead with kisses. "It's gonna be okay. I'm here now," he reassured her, his voice filled with love and determination.

Turning his attention to the neighbor, Travis asked if he had witnessed anything. The neighbor shook his head, expressing his inability to see much beyond the sound of the car speeding away.

Frustration surged through Travis. Clenching his fist, he glanced at Deuce and the other officers present, his anger palpable. "Y'all better catch this son of a bitch before I do!" he declared, his voice laced with resolve.

Grabbing Frankie's hand, Travis led her away from the commotion. They bid farewell to Deuce and made their way home, seeking solace and safety in each other's presence.

Meanwhile, Deuce, deeply affected by the events, made a phone call to one of his colleagues. As he spoke on the phone, his tone was filled with determination.

"What up, man?" he greeted his colleague. "Yeah, this shit just became personal."

Suni walked through the front door, a smile playing on her lips as she recalled the evening she had just spent with the girls. She kicked off her shoes and called out for Blue.

"Hey baby, where are you?" she called, hanging up her coat on the hook by the door.

"I'm in here, sweetheart," Blue's voice floated from their bedroom.

Curiosity piqued, Suni made her way down the dimly lit hallway, her heart racing with anticipation. As she reached the bedroom, she noticed the soft glow of candlelight escaping through the crack. She gently pushed open the door, and her eyes widened in surprise.

The room was transformed into a romantic haven. Candles flickered on every available surface, casting a warm and intimate glow. Red rose petals were scattered across the floor, creating a path that led to the center of the room. Suni stood there, momentarily speechless, taking in the sight before her. The love and effort Blue had put into creating this ambiance overwhelmed her.

"What's all of this?" she asked, her voice getting choked up as she looked around at the lighted candles in the room.

Blue took a step forward, his eyes never leaving Suni's face.

"Nothing special, baby, just because," he said with a smile as he took her hand. "I have a hot bubble bath waiting for you."

Suni hummed in delight. She stood in the doorway, her eyes shocked at the sight before her. The bathroom was transformed into a romantic oasis, with flickering candles casting a warm glow and delicate rose petals scattered across the floor. The air was filled with the scent of lavender, creating an atmosphere of love and tranquility.

Suni undressed and headed for the tub.

"Babe, this is so lovely!" she exclaimed, looking at all the lighted candles and rose petals surrounding the tub. Suni sat in the bathtub, steam rising from the hot water. She smiled mischievously and winked at Blue, causing his heart to skip a beat. Blue couldn't help but return her playful gesture with a soft giggle.

"Come and join me, baby," Suni said, giving Blue a seductive look.

"Of course," he said, gladly accepting the invitation.

Suni and Blue sat together in the warm, soothing water of the tub. As Blue tenderly washed her back, Suni's emotions overcame her, and she finally broke down, sobbing.

Blue immediately pulled Suni closer, wrapping his arms around her. Blue looked at her, concern evident in his eyes.

"Suni, I hate that you're going through this, but I want you to know that I've got you. I'm here for you," he said, his voice filled with love and determination.

Suni sniffled, her tears subsiding for a moment. "I know you do, and I love you so much for it," she said, hugging him tighter. "I do have faith, and I know God is real, and through Him, all things are possible. But sometimes, I just can't help but feel like we won't find her alive."

Blue's heart ached for her, and he fought back tears of his own. "Baby, don't think like that," he said, his voice filled with conviction. "I believe they're going to find her, and you all will be reunited with Billie. So let's claim it right now, okay?"

Suni looked at him, her tears mixing with a glimmer of hope in her eyes.

"Guess what?" Blue said.

"What..." she began to ask, her voice filled with curiosity.

Blue smiled mischievously and rubbed his hands together. "I have a surprise for you, something I think will cheer you up," he said. "I'll be right back."

Blue got out of the tub, wrapping a towel around his waist as he walked into the bedroom. Suni was left in the tub, a mixture of anticipation and wonder filling her mind.

"Hmm..." she murmured, wondering what surprise Blue had in store for her.

Blue stood in the bathroom, holding up a beautiful box that had arrived that day. "This came today," he said, a mixture of excitement and curiosity in his voice.

Suni's eyes widened with anticipation. "Is that what I think it is?" she asked, a smile spreading across her face.

Blue nodded, his own smile mirroring hers.

Suni couldn't contain her excitement and quickly got out of the tub, her wet feet leaving damp footprints on the floor.

"I'm soooo excited!" she exclaimed, jumping up and down with glee. "But wait... they were supposed to call me when my dress came in. I'm very confused!"

Blue picked up the box, noticing the label that read Jax Bridal Boutique.

"Well, it says Jax Bridal Boutique on the box," he said, handing it to Suni. "Regardless, I can't wait to see what's inside."

Suni grinned mischievously and playfully pushed Blue out of the bathroom. "No peeking!" she chuckled. "I'll be right out."

Suni closed the door, leaving Blue waiting in anticipation on the other side.In the silence of the bathroom, Suni picked up the box, her hands trembling with excitement. She smiled, savoring the moment, before finally opening it.

But then, a gut-wrenching scream pierced through the air, echoing through the house. Blue's heart dropped, and he ran towards the bathroom, fear and concern consuming him.

"Baby, what is it?!" he called out, bursting through the door.

He found Suni sitting on the floor, her body shaking, tears streaming down her face. She pointed to the box on the floor, unable to speak.

Blue's eyes fell on the box, and his heart sank. Instead of a dress, there were several newspaper clippings from their high school days. Among them was a picture of Brandy, along with a chilling note written in red ink: "You won't make it to your wedding day, I promise you."

Blue rushed to Suni's side, wrapping his arms around her, trying to offer comfort in the face of such a horrifying discovery.

"Shh, baby, it's okay. I've got you," he whispered, rocking her back and forth as she sobbed uncontrollably.

Their world had been shattered once again, and the threat looming over their lives had become even more sinister.

Teddy sat behind the wheel of her car, leaving the Happy Hour Bar and Grill. She reached for her phone and dialed Cyd's number, eager to share the events of the evening.

The phone rang, and Cyd, just arriving home, answered with a warm hello.

"Hey, baby!" Cyd exclaimed, a smile evident in her voice.

Cyd, holding the door open, greeted Teddy with equal enthusiasm.

"Hey, baby, how did it go with the ladies?" Cyd asked, stepping inside their home.

"Actually, it went pretty well," Teddy replied, her voice filled with satisfaction.

Cyd's face lit up with joy. "That's great, sweetheart! Are you on your way home?"

Teddy nodded, even though Cyd couldn't see her. "Yes, I'll see you soon."

Cyd's voice was filled with warmth. "Okay, honey. Goodbye."

Teddy couldn't help but smile. "Bye, my love."

Both Teddy and Cyd hung up their phones, feeling the love and support that strengthened their bond. In a world filled with uncertainty and challenges, they found solace and comfort in each other's embrace. Together, they would navigate whatever obstacles lay ahead, their love serving as an anchor in the storm.

Cyd, feeling relaxed after a long day at work, decided to pour herself a glass of wine while her favorite jazz song played through their Bluetooth surround sound speakers. With a satisfying pop, she unscrewed the cork and filled her glass, the rich aroma of the wine filling the air.

As she settled onto the couch, Cyd noticed the blinking light on their home answering machine. Swirling the wine in her glass, she pressed the voicemail button and took a sip, preparing herself to listen to the messages.

The first message was from Cyd's mother, a loving check-in from her family. A smile formed on Cyd's face as she listened, comforted by their words.

The second message was for Teddy, from the YMCA, where she coached basketball. It was a reminder about the girls' uniforms being ready, urging

Teddy to get in touch as soon as possible.

Cyd got up from the couch, intending to pour herself another glass of wine. But as she walked towards the kitchen, she was startled by the sound of shattering glass. Her wine glass slipped from her hand, crashing onto the floor. Heart pounding, she rushed back to the couch.

The third message played, and a chill ran down Cyd's spine. A horrific scream filled the room, a voice pleading for help. Tears welled up in Cyd's eyes as she listened, paralyzed by fear.

"Teddy, oh Teddy! Your days are numbered, bitch!" a robotic and sinister voice declared, sending shivers down Cyd's spine. The messages continued, each one more disturbing than the last.

"It's been such a long time. Can't wait until we're reunited. Too bad you won't live to talk about it!" a chilling laugh followed.

The fifth message whispered softly, "Teddy, Teddy," accompanied by heavy breathing that echoed through the room.

Cyd stood there, trembling, her tears flowing freely. The messages had taken a terrifying turn, and the threats felt all too real. Fear gripped her heart as she wondered who could be behind such horrifying messages.

Teddy turned the key in the front door, unlocking it and letting herself inside. The sight of Cyd on the floor, cleaning up broken glass, caught her attention.

"Looks like you had an accident, huh?" Teddy chuckled. "Tell me what happened."

Cyd didn't respond, her gaze fixed on the task at hand. She continued cleaning up the mess without looking up. Concerned, Teddy approached her.

"Cyd, baby, are you okay?" Teddy asked, kneeling down beside her. She gently took the towel out of Cyd's hand. "Look at me and tell me what's wrong."

Cyd stood up and walked over to the answering machine. Without a word, she played the disturbing messages for Teddy. Tears streamed down her face as she listened to the horrifying threats.

As Teddy heard the messages for the first time, fury and rage surged through her. She couldn't contain her anger any longer. In a fit of frustration, she grabbed the answering machine and hurled it against the wall.

Teddy pulled Cyd into a tight embrace, holding her close. "I'm so sorry, Cyd baby," she whispered, her voice filled with remorse.

In the midst of their embrace, Teddy's cell phone began to ring, breaking the tension in the room. She looked at her purse, where the sound was coming from, and felt a mix of apprehension and curiosity.

Teddy cautiously walked towards her ringing cell phone inside her purse. With a mix of apprehension and determination, she answered the call.

"Hello!" Teddy spoke, her voice filled with a mixture of caution and defiance. However, on the other end of the line, she could only hear heavy breathing. Frustrated, she demanded a response.

"Say something, you sick son of a bitch!" Teddy exclaimed. A chilling, robotic laugh echoed through the phone. Unfazed, Teddy continued, "I'm right here! Come and get me, you fucking coward!"

She hung up the phone, but it immediately began to ring again. Teddy hesitated for a moment before picking it up and answering.

"What?" she asked, her voice filled with frustration and anticipation. To her relief, she heard Charlie's voice on the other end.

"Teddy, it's me, Charlie. Are you okay?" Charlie asked, concern evident in her voice.

Teddy let out a sigh of relief. "Yeah, I'm okay. What's up?"

In light of the horrifying events of the past 24 hours and the mandatory stay-at-home order due to the rising virus numbers, the group of ladies and their families decided it was best to go into hiding under police protection. They hoped that this measure would keep them safe from harm and help expedite the resolution of the case.

"It's time, Teddy," Charlie said, her voice filled with determination.

Teddy nodded, even though Charlie couldn't see her. "Yeah, I know."

Time passed, marked by the mounting tension and fear that had enveloped their lives. The decision to go into hiding under police protection was made, and now the ladies and their families were preparing to face an uncertain future.

CHAPTER 7

The next day, Teddy stood at the door of her in-laws' house, clutching her suitcase tightly. Inside, Cyd's parents offered comfort and support. Teddy grabbed her luggage, preparing to say goodbye to Cyd.

"Teddy sniffled, knowing it was time for her to go," she said with a sad face. She hugged Cyd tightly as tears streamed down her cheeks.

"Shush, baby," Teddy whispered. "It's going to be okay." She looked into Cyd's eyes, trying to reassure her. "I'll be back before you know it," she smiled. "In the meantime, you'll be staying with your parents. Mom and Dad will take care of you."

Teddy walked down the steps, turned back, and waved goodbye one last time. As she mumbled the words, "I love you" to Cyd, she got into the waiting van. A police officer opened the door for her, and they drove off.

On the front porch of Suni and Blue's house, they stood, saying their goodbyes.

"I'm going to call you every day," Blue promised, his voice filled with longing. "I can't wait for you to become my wife."

Suni nodded, tears streaming down her face. "Okay," she managed to say amidst her tears.

"I'm happy you're going to be safe," Blue said, his voice filled with love. A black police van pulled up, and Blue walked Suni to the car. He kissed her forehead tenderly.

"Take care of her," he said to the cop.

"I'm on it," the officer replied.

Suni got into the van, and they drove off, leaving Blue standing on the porch, watching them disappear.

Moments later, the front door of Charlie and Bikori's house swung open, and both Charlie and Frankie walked out. Bikori and Travis escorted them to the waiting van.

"You remember what I told you, right?" Travis asked, looking directly into Frankie's eyes.

Frankie nodded, her expression filled with determination.

As they reached the van, Travis's words echoed in Frankie's mind. "Be strong," she whispered to herself.

Charlie and Frankie climbed into the van, ready to face the unknown. Travis closed the door, and the van drove away, leaving Charlie and Frankie's house behind.

The four couples had said their farewells, embarking on a journey filled with uncertainty, hoping to reunite once again. Little did they know that their paths would intertwine, leading them down a treacherous road that would test their strength and love like never before.

Travis and Frankie stood outside the van, their hands tightly intertwined. Travis looked into Frankie's eyes and spoke with a gentle tone.

"I'm just a phone call away," he assured her. "I love you."

Frankie smiled, squeezing his hand. "Love you more."

Bikori approached Charlie, concern evident in her eyes. He gazed deeply into Charlie's eyes and asked, "You good, baby?"

Charlie hesitated for a moment, then nodded. "Yes, I think so," she replied, her voice filled with uncertainty.

"You're going to feel so much better, babe, after talking to the ladies,"

Bikori reassured her.

Charlie stood there, her face filled with nervousness. "I sure hope so," she said quietly.

Bikori locked eyes with Charlie and reminded her, "I'm still here, aren't I?"

Charlie nodded, grateful for Bikori's unwavering support. Both couples shared a final hug before the ladies got into the van. As the van drove off, Teddy, Charlie, Suni, and Frankie waved goodbye, their hearts filled with a mix of hope and trepidation.

Travis was saying his last goodbye to Frankie when his phone suddenly rang. He glanced at the screen and saw the caller ID: Deuce.

Inside the police station, Deuce had a lead in the case and was eager to share the news with Travis.

Travis answered the call, his voice filled with anticipation. "Hello?"

"Hey bro, can you talk?" Deuce's voice came through.

"Yeah, bro, we're good," Travis replied. "Just saying goodbye to Frankie and the ladies."

Deuce chuckled. "Yeah, man, that's good. They're going away for a minute. That's definitely for the best!"

Confusion crept into Travis's voice. "Why? What are you saying?"

Deuce took a deep breath. "Those fingerprints came back, and you're not going to believe this shit!"

Travis's heart raced. "How soon can we meet up?"

"Shit, we can meet up now!" Deuce exclaimed.

"Bet, I'm on my way," Travis said, a mix of excitement and anxiety flooding his thoughts.

In the car, Charlie turned to the ladies, a determined look on her face. She spoke with urgency.

"We have to make one stop before heading to the lake," she informed them, her voice tinged with a sense of purpose.

Curiosity piqued, and the ladies exchanged glances, wondering what awaited them at this unexpected stop. Little did they know that this detour would lead them closer to the truth, unraveling the secrets that had haunted their lives for far too long.

Moments later, the ladies arrived at Bellman's Cemetery. The atmosphere was heavy with dark, brooding clouds, and an eerie stillness hung in the air. The wind howled through the ancient trees, their branches creaking and swaying. Charlie sat in the car, her gaze fixed on a distant grave. Taking a deep breath, she gathered the courage to step out of the car. As she opened the door, Teddy reached out and grabbed her hand.

"Sis, do you need me to go with you?" Teddy asked, concern etched on her face.

"No, this is something I have to do by myself, but thank you," Charlie replied, offering a grateful smile as she exited the car.

The other ladies watched as Charlie made her way toward the grave, their curiosity piqued.

"What is this all about?" Suni asked, her curiosity getting the better of her.

Teddy shook her head. "I don't know, but it's really eating away at her, whatever it is."

Charlie approached Brandy's gravesite. The blowing winds and dark clouds added to the somberness of the moment. Standing before Brandy's tombstone, Charlie fought to maintain her composure, but it proved to be a challenging task. The memories flooded her mind, flashes of confronting Brandy in the gym, seeing her lying in a pool of blood, and Brandy standing on the ledge. Overwhelmed, Charlie finally succumbed to her emotions, breaking down in tears.

"I can't do this," Charlie murmured, shaking her head as she turned to walk back towards the car.

However, something stopped her in her tracks. Clenching her fists and closing her eyes, Charlie took a deep breath. She turned back around, her gaze fixed on Brandy's picture on the tombstone. In that moment, she found the strength to speak her truth.

"Where do I begin?" Charlie's voice quivered, tears streaming down her face. "It's taken me ten years to get here."

Dissolving into memories, Charlie continued, her voice filled with a mix of sadness and remorse.

"Coming here before now would have reminded me that I'm responsible for you being here, and that wasn't something I was able to face until now," Charlie confessed. She took a deep breath and composed herself.

"Do you remember when we first met?" Charlie asked, a hint of nostalgia in her voice. "You thought you were the shiznit when it came to basketball! I just laughed and said, 'You a'ight!'"

Charlie chuckled softly, reminiscing about their closeness in the past.

"We were close back then," she continued. "You were my biggest cheerleader. You told me to always believe in myself because you did and to always put family first."

Charlie stood in front of Brandy's grave, lost in her thoughts. Memories flooded her mind, replaying the moments of their complicated friendship. She daydreamed about Brandy lying on the ground, remembering the hurt and betrayal she felt at the time.

"We went through so much that summer," Charlie spoke softly, her voice tinged with a mix of pain and reflection. "We were friends one minute and enemies the next. I felt betrayed by you, and it took me a while to get over losing a friend. Life was better until the day I found out Salem West was going to play Salem East in the finals. My heart sank."

Charlie took a deep breath, the weight of the past heavy on her shoulders. She continued, tears streaming down her face.

"I knew seeing you after all these years would force me to relive the day my world changed, and I wasn't ready to face that again," she confessed, her voice trembling. "At the time, I thought my world was over because of you, but now I know that wasn't the case. I'm so sorry, Brandy! I regret everything that happened. Only God knows that if I had a chance to go back to that day, I would do things so differently."

As the leaves continued to swirl around her, the wind blowing against her face, Charlie closed her eyes. She turned around and began walking back towards the car, her emotions overwhelming her. But suddenly, she stopped in her tracks, her fist clenched and shaking. She abruptly turned around, her finger pointed towards Brandy's grave, tears streaming down her face.

"I was so angry at you," Charlie yelled, her voice filled with anguish. "You and I both know why, right? If it wasn't for me, you wouldn't be here. It took me a long time to come to grips with that, and there's nothing I can do about it now. If I could go back to that day, seeing you on that ledge, this is what I would say to you."

Charlie's voice softened as she imagined speaking to Brandy.

"Brandy, you are not alone. Please come down. I'm sorry, and I stand with you," she pleaded, her voice filled with regret. "We love you, Brandy, and your future is bright! The world needs you. You are brave and courageous."

With each word, Charlie's tone became more heartfelt, her voice carrying the weight of her own transformation.

"That day changed me, and I am no longer that person because of you," Charlie declared. "So many others are able to live in their truth because of you. How inspiring is that? And it's about time I live in my truth. Yeah, it's time."

Before leaving, Charlie shared the impact Brandy had on her life.

"Before I go, I just wanted you to know that I started a scholarship program in your name called Hope for Girls, the Brandy Alexander Scholarship," she revealed, a hint of pride in her voice. "Me and the ladies created it, and it's going pretty well. I think you would be proud. Thank you for inspiring me."

Wiping the tears from her eyes, Charlie slowly bent down and placed flowers on Brandy's grave. She stood up, taking a deep breath, finding solace in her words. She spoke one last time, her voice filled with a mix of reverence and empowerment.

"Say her name - Brandy Leanne Alexander. Rest in power, beautiful lady," Charlie said, paying her respects before walking away.

As Charlie left the cemetery, a sense of closure and healing began to wash over her, knowing that she had confronted her past and found a way to honor Brandy's memory.

The four ladies arrived at Charlie and Bikori's lake house, their eyes widening in awe as they caught sight of the magnificent white house before them. As they stepped out of the car, their jaws dropped in disbelief, taking in the beauty that surrounded them.

"Man, Charlie, this is beautiful," Teddy exclaimed, marveling at the sight.

Frankie looked around in amazement. "Yeah, I woke up from a nap and landed in paradise. Look at this place!" She swept her eyes across the manicured gardens and the panoramic view of the tranquil lake.

Suni couldn't contain her excitement. "This is the bomb!"

Charlie smiled, feeling proud. "I know, right? Bikori inherited it from his parents."

Teddy pointed down the hill. "What's that down there?"

Charlie followed her gaze. "Oh, that's the pool house. Come on, ladies, if you like the outside, you're definitely going to love the inside."

The ladies made their way inside the lake house, their footsteps echoing on the grand entrance steps. They couldn't help but marvel at the stunning architecture and meticulous attention to detail.

"Whooooeee chile, this place got it going on!" Suni exclaimed, her voice filled with excitement.

Charlie beamed at their reactions. "Well, I'm glad you all like it."

As the ladies continued to explore, their eyes filled with wonder, Charlie's phone rang. She glanced down and saw that it was Bikori calling, a blush creeping onto her face.

"Hello?" Charlie answered, her voice filled with warmth.

"Hey, babe!" Bikori's voice came through the phone, his own excitement evident.

Charlie's smile widened. "Hey, my love, what are you up to?"

"Nothing much, just decided to take a quick jog in the park," Bikori replied, his voice relaxed. "I see you guys made it."

"Yeah, babe, the place looks lovely!" Charlie exclaimed, gratitude filling her voice.

Bikori chuckled. "There's wine and cheese on the counter and food in the fridge."

Charlie walked over to the fridge, her heart fluttering. "When did you have time to do all of this?" she asked, a hint of curiosity in her voice.

Bikori laughed. "I have my ways."

Charlie's eyes glistened with appreciation. "Thank you for all of this, sweetheart."

"You're welcome," Bikori replied, his voice filled with affection. "I will talk to you later. Let Kevin (cop) know if you guys need anything."

"Okay, honey. Goodbye," Charlie said, a tinge of sadness in her voice.

"Goodbye," Bikori responded, and the call ended.

Bikori continued walking in the park, a strange look on his face. Eventually, he stopped and stood still, tears welling up in his eyes. Suddenly, he knelt down in front of what appeared to be Brandy's grave and placed flowers on her tombstone. Kissing Brandy's picture, he sobbed softly.

"I'm so sorry about this, but it will be over soon," Bikori whispered. He stood up and walked away, leaving the grave behind, carrying a heavy secret within him.

CHAPTER 8

The ladies - Charlie, Suni, Teddy, and Frankie - gathered in the cozy family room of the lake house. The sun was starting to set, casting a warm glow over the serene surroundings. They had just finished a delicious catered meal, and now it was time to relax, drink a variety of wines, and reminisce.

Suni, leaning back in her chair, turned to Charlie and asked, "Do you know if we can get local news out here?"

Charlie, sipping her drink, pondered for a moment. "I'm not sure, why?"

Suni sighed, her thoughts on Billie. "Just thinking about Billie, hope we'll have some answers soon."

Teddy, taking a drag from her vape, chimed in. "Shit... You and me both."

Charlie offered reassurance. "The police said they will keep us posted on any updates."

Frankie reminded them of Deuce. "Don't forget we have Deuce too."

A brief silence fell upon the room as the crackling fireplace provided a comforting ambiance. The flickering flames danced in rhythm with the ladies' thoughts, reflecting the shared concern they all felt for their dear friend, Billie.

Suddenly, Charlie jumped up, her eyes sparkling with a glimmer of hope. "In the meantime, let's all stay prayed up. I believe that this is the beginning of new beginnings for us. I just feel it!"

She held up an old yearbook with excitement. Frankie laughed, anticipating the nostalgia that was about to come.

"Oh no," Frankie chuckled. "Girl, uh-uh! Bye Felicia, I'm not trying to go down memory lane. I looked a hot mess back then!"

Suni chimed in, fondly remembering. "You were so cute, and you know it!"

Teddy pointed at a picture of John Mathews in the yearbook. "Oh snap, look at John Mathews!"

Frankie laughed. "Playa, playa!"

Suni added, "Ride or die for his women!"

Teddy smirked mischievously. "Shiiitt... I heard he's still a ride or die!"

Curiosity arose among the ladies as they playfully reminisced about their high school days. Teddy dropped a rumor she had heard.

"Well, I hope this isn't true. However, I did hear something in the streets recently at the barbershop about him donating his plasma to pay one of his chicks' rent!" Teddy laughed, shaking her head.

Frankie reacted with surprise. "Say what?"

Suni burst into laughter. "Now that's a bad bitch!"

The room filled with laughter as they enjoyed each other's company and shared stories. Suddenly, the topic shifted to Charlie's past, and Frankie couldn't help but inquire.

"Charlie, you never talk about your freshman year or even what school you attended. Why is that?"

Teddy, eager for answers, joined in. "What do you have to tell us?"

Charlie stood up, tears welling up in her eyes. She took a sip of her wine and turned toward the ladies.

"I will get into all of that tonight, I promise. But first, let's have some fun," she said, wiping away her tears, determined to enjoy the present moment.

Travis pushed open the heavy glass doors of the 7th District Police Station. The cool air-conditioned interior washed over him, filling his nostrils with the familiar scent of polished wood and faint hints of coffee. The bustling station was abuzz with activity - officers typing on computers, radios crackling with updates, and occasional voices echoing throughout the hallways. Travis made his way toward Sergeant Felicia Ramirez, who was engrossed in paperwork at the desk.

"Hey Fe, is my boy in his office?" Travis asked, pointing towards Deuce's office.

Sergeant Ramirez looked up, chuckling. "Yeah, he's in there. You don't hear him?"

Travis chuckled in response. "Yeah, I do. Thanks, Fe."

Travis walked towards Deuce's office, the sound of Deuce's loud voice yelling at someone on the phone reaching his ears. Deuce noticed Travis and motioned for him to come in and have a seat.

Inside the office, Deuce was still engaged in a heated phone conversation about his trash services.

"I didn't ask to have my services changed!" Deuce exclaimed, frustration evident on his face.

The customer service representative calmly responded, "Sir, I am aware of this and apologize. However, Waste Collections no longer services your area. Tucker's Trash Company does."

Deuce threw his hands in the air, exasperated. "So, you're telling me there's nothing I can do about this?"

The customer service representative replied sarcastically, "Sir, you can move."

Deuce sighed, shaking his head. "Well, damn! Trust me, if I could, I would."

As the call ended, Deuce muttered, "Thank you for nothing, have a good day. Evil ass!" He hung up the phone, his frustration lingering.

Travis couldn't help but laugh. "Hey, man, what was that all about?"

Deuce chuckled in response. "Some bullshit."

Deuce pulled his seat back and sat down, gathering a file and loading up his computer. He turned to Travis, ready to get down to business.

"Let's just get down to business," Deuce said. He turned on his computer and began explaining the fingerprint process.

"You see, when the forensic department runs fingerprints, they use what we call the ACE-V process, which involves analysis, comparison, and verification," Deuce explained. "This method helps determine the print's match. The fingerprints were put into our database, and this is what we came up with."

Deuce turned the computer around towards Travis, revealing a picture of a person. Travis scooted up closer to Deuce's desk, his eyes narrowing as he focused on the image.

"Wait a minute," Travis spoke, his voice filled with confusion. "Is that who I think it is?"

Deuce confirmed, "Yeah, that's homeboy from East!"

Travis contemplated, "Yeah, but what would be the motive?"

Deuce shrugged. "Shit... who knows?"

Travis continued to stare at the picture, his mind filled with questions. Deuce shared some surprising information.

"You know the craziest thing about all of this," Deuce began, "his record is clean, and we can't find anything on him for the last nine years! It's like he vanished into thin air! I mean, the shit is mind-boggling to me."

Travis was intrigued and asked, "So if that's the case, how were you able to link him to the crime scene? How were you guys able to identify his prints?"

Deuce leaned back in his chair, scratching his head. "Man... all I can say is thank God for the MCAT."

Travis questioned, "MCAT? What's that?"

Deuce explained, "The Medical College Admissions Test. Apparently, old dude applied to medical school, and in order to register for this exam, you have to have your fingerprints taken."

Travis absorbed the information, his curiosity growing. "We checked with the medical board, hoping he was registered as a physician somewhere, but we got nothing! Even his social media page is shut down, and because it was a private page, I have to wait for the court order to come back to open it."

Travis shook his head in disbelief. "Damn, what does this mean? 'Cause this shit is hard to swallow."

Deuce acknowledged the challenge ahead. "It means we have our work cut out for us, shit. That's what this means."

Travis wanted to update the ladies but understood the need for discretion. "Can I tell the ladies we have a break in the case?"

Deuce advised, "Naw, man, not yet. But I will keep you posted. I don't know how yet, but we're gonna figure this shit out. Please believe that."

Travis nodded in agreement, acknowledging the ongoing investigation.

"I'll hit you up tomorrow," Deuce said.

Travis responded with a simple "Okay," as the scene faded out.

Charlie's weariness hit her like a ton of bricks. She stumbled, her legs threatening to give way beneath her, and she sank down onto a nearby chair. The weight of fatigue settled over her, and her limbs protested every movement. She mumbled to herself, "Oh boy, I'm really tired... I guess I'm getting too old." Chuckling, she trailed off, her words dissolving into a yawn that overtook her. Her eyes drooped, and the urge to rest consumed her.

Frankie, sitting nearby, couldn't help but empathize with Charlie's exhaustion. She started yawning as well, stretching her arms and rubbing her eyes. The weariness seeped into her bones.

"Me too," Frankie admitted, yawning. "Seems like we're all getting old and could use a good night's rest." She attempted to chuckle.

Meanwhile, Teddy, who had been standing at the window, suddenly felt a wave of dizziness wash over her. She clutched her head, momentarily disoriented, and made her way to the nearby couch for support.

Teddy remarked, "Either I'm just weak, or that is some potent-ass wine!" She let out another yawn.

Suni, sitting on the toilet in the bathroom, struggled to keep her eyes open. Despite her fatigue, she declared, "I don't know about you guys, but I'm ready to party some more!" She danced her way back to the family room, only to find the rest of the ladies passed out.

Suni sighed, "I knew y'all couldn't hang with me!" Chuckling, she admitted, "I'm thirsty. Let me get some water." Suni walked towards the kitchen, but the room started spinning. Her steps grew shorter and shorter, and she stumbled to the fridge to get some water. As she struggled to pour the water, she realized she needed to sit down. Suni attempted to place the glass on the counter but failed, ultimately passing out and dropping the glass on the floor, shattering it.

In the dimly lit room of an undisclosed location, the person of interest sat in a creaky old rocking chair, their face hidden within the shadowy depths. A single camera, positioned on a tripod in the corner, diligently captured their every move and expression. Their eyes, piercing and cold, stared directly into the lens, creating an eerie atmosphere.

With a chilling robotic tone that sent shivers down the spine, the person let out a haunting laugh devoid of any genuine amusement. The sound reverberated through the room, bouncing off the bare walls, intensifying the unsettling atmosphere. As the laughter subsided, the person leaned closer to the camera, their face gradually coming into clearer view. Their voice, still tinged with the robotic tone, uttered the words, "Nighty night, bitches," punctuated by a disturbing exaggerated wave of their hand.

Outside someone's house on a bright day, Deuce stood with a piece of paper in his hand, carefully studying the address before him. He nodded, confirming that he had arrived at the correct location. Determinedly, he approached the porch and rang the doorbell, cautiously watching his surroundings. An older lady answered the door, her voice trembling with uncertainty.

"Can I help you?" she asked, her hands shaking.

"Yes, ma'am," Deuce replied, his tone calm and professional. "My name is Roman. I'm a detective with the 7th District. I'm looking for Kamron Dior. I do believe he's your son."

The older lady's confusion grew as she shook her head vigorously. "Who are you? What do you want? I don't have a son by that name!"

Deuce glanced at the house and then back at the paper in his hand, his eyebrows furrowing. "Are you sure? When I ran a background check on Kamron, this address came up with you listed as his next of kin."

An expression of frustration crossed the older lady's face. "I just told you, I don't have a son! Please leave my home."

Deuce attempted to reason with her, hoping to find some answers, but she remained resolute, closing the door in his face. He stood there for a moment, putting his hands on his hips, contemplating the situation. "Damn. What the fuck?" he muttered, looking back at the house with a mix of confusion and determination.

CHAPTER 9

The ladies awoke to a terrifying reality. As their eyes fluttered open, they realized they were bound and gagged, their muffled screams strangled by the rags tightly fastened around their mouths. Panic set in as they struggled against their restraints, their eyes wide with fear.

Frankie, her heart pounding in her chest, managed to look up and noticed another person tied up with her, their head down, preventing her from seeing their face at the moment. Desperation filled her eyes as she tried to catch the attention of the other ladies, her voice stifled by the cloth in her mouth.

With a flicker of movement, the person beside Frankie began to stir. Slowly, their head lifted, revealing their face. It was Billie! Frankie's anguished screams turned into muffled cries of joy as she pointed toward Billie, urging the other ladies to look. Shock and love filled their eyes as they realized their beloved friend was also trapped with them.

Just then, a flashing light from the ceiling caught their attention. A voice, cold and robotic, echoed through the room.

"Well, well, well... Looks like the starting five are all back together again," the voice sneered sarcastically. It continued, "I added some music for your enjoyment and pleasure!" The sound of familiar tunes filled the air, but instead of bringing comfort, it only added to their unease.

"Y'all hold tight," the voice taunted. "I will be down shortly to introduce myself."

Meanwhile, outside the lake house, Kevin reclined in his car seat, overlooking the serene beauty of the lake. He spoke casually on the phone with a colleague, the sound of nature's tranquility providing a soothing backdrop.

Kevin chuckled, a puff of smoke escaping from his lips as he enjoyed his joint. The aroma of marijuana mingled with the crisp scent of pine in the air. His voice laced with contentment, he remarked, "Man, it doesn't get any better than this!"

His colleague, envious of Kevin's idyllic setting, replied, "You lucky bastard! I wish it was me."

Smiling, Kevin took another drag from his joint, relishing the moment. "I can do this shit all day, every day!" he declared, exhaling slowly. Nature's beauty enveloped him, momentarily shielding him from the chaos of the outside world.

As Kevin's gaze wandered, he noticed a peculiar flashing light in his rearview mirror emanating from the pool house. His relaxed demeanor turned to confusion and concern.

"What the hell?" Kevin muttered, his attention now fully captured by the mysterious light.

Concerned for Kevin's well-being, his colleague asked, "You good, Kevin?"

Kevin hesitated, a knot forming in his stomach. "Yeah... Man, let me call you back," he responded, ending the conversation.

With the phone call concluded, Kevin stubbed out the joint in the car's ashtray and instinctively reached for his gun. Exiting the car, he walked towards the pool house, a sense of unease gnawing at him. The feeling of being watched intensified, causing him to pause and scan his surroundings.

He took a final glance to the side, his peripheral vision capturing a glimpse of movement. A mix of anticipation and trepidation flooded his senses. With a heavy breath, he abruptly turned around, his gun pointed outward. And there, standing before him, was a familiar face.

"Man, you scared the shit out of me!" Kevin exclaimed, his voice filled with both relief and surprise.

But before Kevin could fully process the encounter, he was struck on the head with a heavy object. Darkness consumed him as he collapsed to the ground, unconscious. Unbeknownst to him, the assailant continued towards the pool house, leaving Kevin behind.

Inside the pool house, Bikori unlocked the door, allowing himself entry. The heavy creaking of the door echoed through the room as it swung shut behind him. He trod lightly, his footsteps almost imperceptible, as he made his way toward the bedroom.

Standing at the threshold, Bikori observed a person of interest sitting in the room, fixated on the live camera feed displaying the captive ladies. Their face remained hidden, shrouded in mystery. Slowly, Bikori approached from behind and tapped the person on the shoulder, startling them.

A startled scream escaped their lips as they jumped up from their seat, revealing their identity. It was Mille, the wedding planner. Her wide eyes reflected a mixture of fear and surprise.

"Sorry for that," Bikori apologized, his voice carrying a hint of remorse.

Shaking off the fright, Mille quickly composed herself and inquired, "Did you take care of the guard?"

Bikori nodded, a touch of sadness crossing his face. "Yes, I think so."

Peering at the captive ladies on the camera feed, Mille assessed their condition, her expression one of concern.

"How are they?" Bikori asked.

"Okay, I guess," she responded hesitantly, her voice filled with uncertainty.

Bikori made a request, his tone firm yet tinged with vulnerability. "Please take the rags out of their mouths."

Caught off guard by the unexpected demand, Mille's anger flared. She shot Bikori an angry look and stormed out of the room, forcefully bumping into his shoulder. Bikori stood there, silently watching the ladies on the camera feed, his gaze filled with a mix of determination and concern.

As Mille continued her heated argument with Bikori, her phone rang, shattering the tense atmosphere. She glanced down at the screen, momentarily distracted from the escalating confrontation.

"Hey Mama, what's up? Is everything okay?" Mille answered, her voice laced with worry.

On the other end of the line, Mama-Mrs. Dior's voice crackled with concern, questioning Mille about a detective who had come searching for her son. The realization of potential trouble hung heavy in the air.

Mille reassured her mother, her voice trembling slightly. "Everything is fine. Did you say anything?"

Mama-Mrs. Dior denied any involvement, expressing her concern for Mille's safety. Doubt crept into Mille's voice as she affirmed her well-being, promising to call her mother later. The conversation ended, leaving Mille with a lingering unease.

"And Mama..." Mille hesitated for a moment, her voice filled with unspoken fears.

Mama-Mrs. Dior and Mille exchanged heartfelt words over the phone, their voices filled with emotion.

"I love you!" Mille choked up, tears welling in her eyes.

Mama-Mrs. Dior responded with a smile in her voice, "I love you more."
With their love reaffirmed, they bid each other farewell and ended the call, the connection between them remaining strong despite the distance.

The dimly lit room pulsated with fear as the ladies sat, their gazes fixed on the light descending from the top of the stairs. An air of anticipation mingled with trepidation as the door creaked open, casting a brighter glow upon the scene. Footsteps echoed, each one growing louder and more pronounced, intensifying the tension that gripped their hearts. What awaited them at the top of the stairs?

The sound of footsteps grew nearer, reverberating through the room, causing the ladies' breathing to quicken. Wide-eyed, they exchanged glances, their expressions reflecting a mix of fear and curiosity. And then, a figure clad in all black, wearing a mask, emerged at the bottom of the steps. A shroud of silence enveloped the room as the mysterious person paced back and forth in front of each captive lady.

One by one, the ladies felt the tightness of their gags loosen as the person unbound them. Still, no words were spoken, only an unsettling presence lingering in the air. Their eyes followed the figure as it ascended the steps, closing the door behind them, leaving the ladies bewildered and filled with questions.

Teddy, unable to contain her frustration, demanded answers, her voice laced with anger and desperation. "Hey, what is this shit about? Who the fuck are you, and what do you want from us?"

Silence was the response as the figure looked at each lady, their eyes piercing through the dimly lit room. Without uttering a word, they turned and walked away, leaving the ladies to ponder their fate.

But Charlie couldn't let them leave without a plea. "Please wait!" she called out, her voice trembling with a mix of fear and urgency.

To everyone's surprise, the figure halted, turning to face Charlie, their masked visage peering back at her. The weight of the moment hung heavy in the air as if the answers they sought were just beyond their grasp.

Frustration seeped from Teddy's voice as she unleashed her fury, hoping to elicit a response. "FUCK, man! Show yourself, you fucking coward! Show your face!"

The tension grew, the ladies urging Teddy to stop, fearing the consequences of her actions. Yet, she persisted, screaming into the void, her voice reverberating through the room.

Finally, the door creaked open once more, and a shadowy figure emerged at the top of the stairs. The ladies strained to catch a glimpse of their tormentor, their eyes fixated on the flickering silhouette cast upon the wall. With measured steps, the figure descended, eventually coming to a standstill before the ladies.

Fear etched across their faces, they all watched intently, except for Teddy, whose defiance masked her trepidation. The figure moved closer, standing directly in front of Teddy, their presence looming over her.

"What? I'm not afraid of you, fucking coward!" Teddy boldly challenged. "Show your face. I dare you."

Unfazed, the figure shifted their attention to Charlie, who pleaded for an explanation. "What is this all about? Please, tell us what you want."

Suni's voice trembled with desperation as she added, "We'll give you whatever you want. Just please don't hurt us."

Frankie, her voice shaking, ventured further. "Can you at least tell us if this is just a random robbery? Or is this personal?"

Something about Frankie's words struck a chord, causing the figure to move towards her, pulling off the mask to reveal their identity. The shock that washed over Charlie's face mirrored the revelation before her.

"Mille, is that you?" Charlie stammered, her voice filled with disbelief.

A smirking Mille confirmed her identity. "Yes, it's me," she replied, satisfaction filled in her eyes.

Frankie's confusion lingered as she tried to make sense of the situation unfolding before her.

Teddy's voice cut through the air with recognition. "Yo, that's that bitch from the wedding!"

Charlie, still bewildered, questioned Mille, "What is this all about? What did I ever do to you?"

Mille's response struck a chord, her voice filled with a mix of anger and resentment. "It's not what you did to me, but what you did to us!"

Charlie's confusion deepened. "Us? Who's us?"

Mille raised her voice, shouting up the stairs, "Come on down, baby."

The ladies turned their heads, their expressions a mix of fear and curiosity, as the person slowly descended the steps. Each heavy breath filled the room, the tension thickening.

"It's okay, come on down," Mille reassured the person.

And then, with a gasp of realization, Charlie's voice trembled, "Kori?"

The figure was revealed as Kori, causing Charlie to gasp and breathe heavily in shock.

"Yes, it's me, Charlie," Kori confirmed, his voice filled with a mix of pain and desperation.

Charlie pleaded with Kori, her voice quivering. "Baby, what's going on? What is all of this about? Please talk to me."

Mille walked over to Kori, wrapping her arms around his shoulders, urging him to explain. "Tell her, baby," she said softly.

Charlie, still in shock, looked at the necklace hanging around Kori's neck. Her face contorted with fear as if she had seen a ghost. Her voice trembled as she asked, "Where did you get that necklace from, Kori?"

Kori, breathing heavily, revealed the necklace that read "Family First." Charlie's mind raced as she had flashbacks of seeing Brandy lying on the ground with the same necklace.

"Brandy was my sister," Kori confessed, shocking all five ladies.

Frankie's voice filled with concern, "Oh no!"

Charlie, distraught, tears streaming down her face, couldn't comprehend the situation. "Your sister? No... how?"

In a daze, Charlie had another flashback, recalling a flirtatious conversation with Brandon (Brandy) from their past.

Brandon asked, "Do you have any siblings?"

Charlie flirtatiously replied, "Nope, do you?"

Brandon blushed, rubbing his basketball. "Yeah... a brother."

Charlie snapped out of her thoughts, staring at Kori. She pleaded, "Why are you doing this? Why do you want to hurt me?" Her words were interrupted by her sobbing.

Kori stepped closer, his face filled with anger. "Hurt you? Bitch, my sister is dead because of you! Because of you, she took her own life! If it wasn't for you, she would still be alive today."

Charlie sobbed, her voice choked with guilt. "Kori, I never meant for any of this to happen!"

Teddy, looking at Charlie, asked a pressing question. "Did you know she had a brother?"

Charlie, tears streaming down her face, shook her head. "No, I didn't know at that time."

Kori, filled with resentment, responded, "Well, now you know!"

Teddy interjected, her voice probing. "If you were her brother, then why didn't you attend East like she did?"

Kori walked over towards Teddy, frustration evident in his voice. He replied, "It was Brandy's dream to play for that coach at that school, not mine."

Suni couldn't contain her frustration any longer. "Where were you when all this was going on?"

Bikori's voice trembled with sorrow. "I was at a program in Chicago called 'Hit the Ground Running' for future black engineers. Our plane was delayed. This is partially my fault as well. I should have gotten there in time to save her." He sobbed, overwhelmed by guilt.

Charlie's confusion deepened as she interjected, "But wait, you're a doctor, not an engineer!"

In a flashback, Charlie remembered a conversation with Bikori when they first met.

In the coffee shop, Bikori approached her with a friendly smile. "Well, if it isn't the famous Charlie Morrison, nurse practitioner, and blogger."

Charlie, puzzled, asked, "Do I know you?"

Bikori chuckled. "No, not personally, but I am a huge fan. Can I join you for coffee?"

Charlie blushed and agreed, engaging in conversation during their coffee break.

"Did you always want to be a doctor?" Charlie asked.

Bikori shook his head. "Naw, someone that mattered to me wanted to be a doctor. I'm just carrying on her dream."

Attempting to change the subject, Bikori turned the focus to Charlie. "But enough about me, what about you? Majoring in nursing with a minor in psychology? What's up with that?" she chuckled. "Just like you, I was inspired by someone once close to me as well," Charlie replied.

Charlie had another realization, a memory from the coffee shop conversation. She looked at Bikori and asked, "That day in the coffee shop, it wasn't a coincidence, was it?"

Mille chimed in, chuckling. "Hell naw! Tell them, baby."

Bikori confirmed, "No, it wasn't."

Desperation filled Charlie's voice as she pleaded, "Why go this far? What is it that you want from me? I love you, Kori. I'm not the girl I was in high school. You have to believe me."

Mille scoffed, rejecting Charlie's plea. "We ain't buying it, girlfriend."

Teddy's patience ran thin. "Sorry, bitch! Who are you, and what do you have to do with all of this?"

Mille confronted Teddy, getting in her face. "I'm your worst nightmare, trick!" She dumped water on Teddy, provoking her.

Teddy, shaking the water off, fumed, "If I could get up from here, I would beat your motherfuckin' ass!"

Mille taunted her, confident in her power. "No, you wouldn't. I gave you that same chance in high school."

Curiosity sparked in Teddy's eyes. "High school?"

Teddy's face transformed with revelation, and she exclaimed, "Damn, y'all! It's Kamron!"

Shock rippled through the room as the ladies processed the truth.

Mille paced back and forth, looking at each of them. "Yeah, it's me, bitches. I can't believe I drugged all y'all asses down by myself, especially your big ass, Teddy." She laughed. "I guess I can thank the Beach Body workout series for keeping a bitch in shape. Brandy was my best friend, so all you bitches have to pay."

Charlie's voice quivered with despair. "This is a nightmare."

Bikori corrected her. "No, it became a nightmare the day she met you at camp."

Teddy was taken aback. "Camp?"

Frankie, desperate for answers, implored, "What is he talking about? Somebody, please tell us something."

Charlie sat there in a daze, her mind overwhelmed.

Billie spoke up, recalling Brandy's final request. "Before Brandy jumped, she said for you to tell us why you hated her."

Bikori looked into Charlie's eyes, his voice stern. "You mean you haven't told them?"

Charlie's head hung low as she took a deep breath. "No," she admitted, her voice heavy.

Bikori yelled at Charlie, his frustration boiling over. "Tell them!"

Charlie mustered the strength to speak. "Okay, I will." She paused, gathering her thoughts, before continuing. "He was a he before he was a she. We met at a basketball camp one summer. He was attractive and smart. We became close, like best friends. We even lost our virginity to each other." Charlie's voice trembled as she thought back to that time. "It was the happiest day of my life. I felt so special. But a week later, when I went to Brandon's cabin looking for him, I got a little more than I had bargained for."

Frankie, bewildered, pressed for clarification. "What do you mean?"

Charlie's tears flowed uncontrollably as she revealed the painful memory. "I found him making out with some guy up against the wall. He saw me, and I took off running and crying! I felt so betrayed. He apologized and told me he never meant to hurt me, but I wasn't listening. I was devastated."

Bikori spoke up, acknowledging the truth. "Yes, she told me everything. She didn't mean to hurt you; she was just confused at that time. But you couldn't let it go. She was so afraid to play you in that championship, but I told her that enough time had passed and surely you had forgotten all about her. But no, you had not moved on."

Teddy's voice filled with incredulity as she tried to process the situation. "Soooooo... let me get this straight. You wanted revenge that bad that you went as far as marrying Charlie?"

Bikori didn't hesitate in his response. "Yes, revenge and to take her money. But then, it wasn't even about the money. I just wanted you to pay." He looked into Charlie's eyes, a mix of anger and pain reflecting in his gaze.

Charlie interjected, her voice trembling. "But babe, you knew in my grandfather's will that the money wouldn't go to my spouse even in death."

Mille couldn't resist a smirk. "Yeah, but that damn interest on the accounts is sitting on swole." She rolled her eyes, clearly amused by the situation.

Bikori snapped at Mille, his frustration evident. "Shut up, Kam!"

Mille shrugged, unbothered. "I'm just sayin'."

Teddy shook her head in disbelief. "Damn! You just can't make this shit up."

Charlie pleaded with Bikori, her voice filled with desperation. "Kori, baby, listen to me. If I could change everything, I would. I've lived the last 10 years of my life doing right by Brandy. We all have." Her eyes scanned all the girls, seeking understanding.

Bikori remained unconvinced. "I don't believe you."

Charlie persisted, her voice trembling with sincerity. "Listen to me, Kori. I love you, and I know you love me. You just have to believe me."

Mille interjected, shutting down Charlie's plea. "Girl shut the hell up. It's over for all you guys."

Frankie, puzzled, asked, "What do you mean?"

88

Mille's tone turned chilling as she revealed her intentions. "I mean, say your goodbyes because you guys won't make it out of here alive. I swear that on everything I own."

Teddy, not willing to back down, confronted Mille. "Killing us will not bring Brandy back, okay? Please let us go. If I'm gonna die, I want to know how."

Frankie, alarmed, pleaded with Teddy. "Teddy, what are you doing?"

Teddy stood her ground. "No, if I have to die, I at least want to know how."

Mille smirked as she divulged her plan. "We're going to make it look like a robbery and set the house on fire with you guys in it." She laughed, a chilling sound echoing through the room. "Whooeee... chile, burn bitches burn!"

Mille's relentless comments were met with Bikori's stern response. "Mille, shut up!"

Mille scoffed but didn't argue further. "Well, it's true shit!"

Bikori turned to Charlie with a pained expression on his face. "I'm sorry. It didn't have to be this way," he said to her before starting to walk up the steps.

Charlie couldn't bear to let him go. "We need you!" she yelled, desperation lacing her voice.

Bikori turned around, facing Charlie once more. "What did you say?"

Charlie closed her eyes, took a deep breath, and spoke with heavy emotion. "I said... we need you."

Bikori questioned her further. "Who is 'we'?"

Charlie's mind flooded with flashbacks, recalling a conversation with her aunt at the wedding and images of her little cousin Bella dancing. She sobbed hysterically, also remembering lying in a hospital bed, screaming as she gave birth to a baby girl.

Confused and angry, Bikori demanded answers. "What the hell are you saying?"

Through tears, Charlie revealed the truth. "I'm saying... little Bella, the flower girl, is my daughter and your niece."

The shock on everyone's faces was palpable, unable to believe the revelation that had just been disclosed.

Bikori's anger flared as he looked at Charlie, denying the truth. "No! You're a fucking liar!"

Charlie pleaded with him, her voice filled with sincerity. "No, baby, it's true. I got pregnant that summer. She's your niece. Please believe me," she sobbed.

Frankie couldn't hold back her own tears. "Charlie, is that why you didn't attend West your freshman year?"

Charlie nodded through her tears. "Yes, that's the reason."

Mille, unwilling to accept the revelation, interjected. "Don't believe her, baby! The bitch is lying!"

Teddy silenced Mille with a stern command. "Shut the fuck up!"

Bikori remained unconvinced, declaring his disbelief. "I don't believe you. I've got to go." Both Bikori and Mille headed up the stairs.

Charlie screamed after Bikori as he ascended. "I love you!" she cried out.

The remaining ladies gathered around Charlie, attempting to console her as she continued to cry.

Frankie expressed her remorse. "I'm so sorry."

Teddy chimed in, supportive of her sister. "Yeah, sis, I hate that you had to go through all that shit alone. But we're here now, and this shit isn't over." She looked up towards the top of the stairs with determination.

Charlie spoke up, burdened with guilt. "I'm sorry I got you guys all involved in this." She felt remorseful for dragging her friends into the turmoil.

Billie offered solace. "This is nobody's fault. Let's just pray. That's all we can do right now." All the ladies nodded in unison, finding solace in the power of prayer.

CHAPTER 10

Bikori sat alone in the dimly lit room, engrossed in his laptop, watching the ladies on the surveillance camera. Mille approached him, noticing him focused on Brandy's scholarship page that Charlie and the girls had created.

Mille couldn't contain her anger and disbelief. "Wait a minute, please tell me you're not falling for her? Let's not forget that because of her, you lost a sister, and I lost a best friend. We're not letting that shit ride!" Her head shook with frustration.

Mille's hands trembled as she grabbed Bikori's face, her fingers digging into his cheeks. Bikori stood there in silence, seemingly lost in his thoughts. Mille's eyes bore into his, filled with desperation and longing.

"Look at me," she pleaded, her voice quivering. "Do you love her?"

Bikori pulled away from her, his gaze distant as he struggled to meet Mille's eyes. "I don't know. Just let me think, okay?" He grabbed his head, clearly conflicted.

Mille's emotions overflowed as she cried. She held onto Bikori, whispering through her tears. "What about me? What about you?" Bikori asked, his voice choked with emotion. "I have loved you, been in love with you since high school. Can't you see that?" She sobbed, wiping her nose.

Bikori's face twisted with hurt and confusion. He pushed Mille away gently. "I'm so sorry," he said, his voice filled with confusion. "I never meant to hurt you. And besides, I'm not that type of person. I don't get down like that."

Mille's eyes widened in disbelief as she continued to sob. "What the hell do you mean? Not that type of person? I am a woman!" She ran off, leaving Bikori stunned.

Bikori let out a frustrated exclamation and kicked the trash can in his path. He found Mille sitting alone, and he approached her, filled with regret.

"I'm sorry, okay?" he said, trying to convey his sincerity. Mille wiped her tears, accepting his apology. "It's cool," she replied. "Can we just stay focused and do what the hell we set out to do? Besides, there's no turning back now."

Bikori chimed in, his face displaying a mix of hesitation. "Yeah, you're right," he agreed.

Mille held Bikori's hands, her voice filled with determination. "Look, whatever this is that you think you feel for her, brush that shit off, and let's finish what we started."

Deuce sat in his small office at the police station, his excitement palpable as he just received the approved warrant to access Kamron's deleted private social media account. The dimly lit room echoed with the sound of his tapping fingers on the desk, a nervous energy coursing through him. His eyes were fixed on the computer screen, waiting for it to finish loading up.

Taking a sip from his can of coke, the carbonation tickled his throat as he tried to calm his racing thoughts. The anticipation was barely contained within him. Finally, the screen blinked to life, casting a glow on his face.

"Okay, let's see what the hell is going on with you," Deuce muttered, his voice filled with determination.

As the computer loaded Kamron's social media account, Deuce's eyes scanned the screen, quickly catching sight of the last post. His brows furrowed in confusion as he read the caption, "Goodbye Kamron!"

"What the hell does that mean? 'Goodbye Kamron!'" Deuce wondered aloud, his tone laced with intrigue.

With a deep breath, he continued scrolling through the account, delving into Kamron's past. The screen displayed a collection of photos and messages, each one offering a glimpse into Kamron's life. One particular picture caught Deuce's attention—it was a photo of Kamron standing alongside his mother at his graduation. The caption expressed gratitude for her unwavering love and support.

Deuce's lips curled into a smirk, a sense of revelation washing over him. "So, you lied to me, Mrs. Dior. Well, let's just find out why, shall we?"

With newfound determination, Deuce continued his exploration of Kamron's social media page. As he scrolled through the pictures, a series of images depicting Kamron and Brandy together caught his eye. They radiated happiness and friendship, accompanied by captions expressing their deep bond. One photo even highlighted their shared support for LGBTQ rights.

"Okay, now we're getting somewhere," Deuce muttered, a spark of excitement in his eyes.

His fingers danced across the keyboard as he delved deeper into the social media account. Among the posts, Deuce stumbled upon a newspaper clipping that grabbed his attention—a tragic story about a promising student named Brandy who had taken her own life after being bullied at a basketball game.

Deuce's heart raced as he absorbed the details, his mind working to piece together the puzzle. His eyes darted across the screen, searching for more clues. Another photo emerged, capturing Kamron consoling a grieving individual at Brandy's burial site. The sorrowful moment froze in time as Brandy's casket was lowered into the grave.

Wide-eyed and breathless, Deuce focused on the figure being comforted. Something within him stirred, a realization dawning upon him.

"Naw, naw, I know this is not... who I think it is?" Deuce muttered, his voice filled with disbelief and confusion.

As he continued scrolling through the account, he stumbled upon another intriguing photo—a newspaper article featuring twin brothers who had achieved perfect scores on their ACT exams.

"Oh shit," Deuce exclaimed, his voice trembling with a mix of shock and realization.

Realizing the gravity of the situation, Deuce immediately reached for his phone. With trembling fingers, he dialed Travis' number, urgency evident in his actions.

"Hey, man, call the ladies' family and meet me at the station. I've found something, and this shit is huge," Deuce said quickly, his words overflowing with excitement and a sense of urgency.

The scene shifted to Travis speeding down the highway with Deuce in the passenger seat. Blue and Cydney sat in the back, their expressions a mix of concern and curiosity.

"How are we going to get in? This is a gated community," Deuce questioned, his voice filled with determination.

Travis glanced at him with a confident smile, his grip tightening on the steering wheel. "Trust me, we'll find a way."

As they sped towards their destination, the anticipation grew, the weight of their discoveries hanging in the air. The secrets that lay within Kamron's social media account promised to unveil the truth they had been seeking.

Bikori sat alone in the dimly lit room, his gaze fixed on the surveillance footage of the ladies. Memories of his wedding day flooded his mind, intertwining with images of Bella dancing and playing. Lost in thought, he failed to notice Mille's presence until she found him.

Mille approached Bikori, a sense of urgency in her voice. "It's time, Bikori," she declared, her words tinged with both determination and fear. In her hands, she held a container of gasoline, its pungent scent filling the room.

Without hesitation, Mille struck a match and tossed it into the air. The flame landed on the floor, igniting a blaze that quickly consumed the room. She grabbed Bikori's arm, urging him to leave.

"We have to get out of here!" Mille exclaimed, her voice a mixture of urgency and desperation. Bikori glanced back at the ladies on the camera one last time before running out the door, Mille by his side.

Meanwhile, in the basement, the remaining ladies began to sense the danger. Teddy, with her keen sense of smell, detected the smoke wafting down the stairs.

"Do you all smell that?" Teddy questioned, her voice tinged with concern as she sniffed the air.

Frankie's eyes widened as she saw smoke emerging from upstairs. "Shit! There's smoke coming from upstairs," she exclaimed, her voice filled with alarm.

Suni, overwhelmed with emotion, began crying hysterically, seeking solace in her faith. "Jesus, help us," she pleaded, her words choked with tears.

Charlie, consumed by guilt, sobbed uncontrollably. "I'm so sorry I got you all involved in this," she lamented, her voice filled with remorse.

Teddy, determined to free Billie, tried to untie her hands, but her efforts proved unsuccessful. Frustration overwhelmed her, and she cursed in exasperation. The smoke grew thicker, and Billie's coughing became more intense.

"Fuck, fuck, fuck!" Teddy screamed in frustration, her voice echoing with desperation. The ladies' pleas for help grew louder as they struggled to breathe.

Outside, Bikori and Mille stood in front of the pool house, the flames growing larger before their eyes. Mille reached out, grabbing Bikori's arms, pleading with him to leave.

"Come on, we have to get out of here," Mille implored, her voice filled with urgency. Bikori, lost in a daze, suddenly pushed Mille away and yelled, "No, no. This isn't right!" He took off running back towards the pool house, with Mille chasing after him.

Desperation filled the air as Bikori raced towards the basement door, screaming Charlie's name. He fought through the fire and smoke, determined to reach the ladies as the flames encroached upon them.

Mille, struggling to find Bikori amidst the smoke, screamed and cried out, desperately calling for him. Her voice trembled with fear and sorrow. But Bikori's focus remained on rescuing Charlie. Mille's pleas for help fell on deaf ears as he pressed forward.

Suddenly, Mille found herself surrounded by fire, trapped with no escape. Desperate, she cried out to Bikori, "Please... help me!" But his attention was drawn to another sound—the screams of a woman in distress.

Bikori hesitated for a moment, torn between the two, before deciding to turn back towards the basement steps. But before he could reach Mille, an explosion shook the house. The basement steps collapsed, preventing his rescue attempt.

Tears welled up in Bikori's eyes as he whispered, "I'm sorry, Mille," before turning his attention to rescuing the trapped ladies.

Bikori quickly located Charlie and set to work uncuffing her, his urgency evident in his actions. Slapping her gently across the face, he pleaded, "Charlie, baby, wake up. Is everybody okay?"

Charlie, struggling with the smoke, coughed and replied, "I think so. Please, hurry and uncuff us. Billie is not okay!" Her voice carried a sense of urgency and concern.

Bikori wasted no time as he freed all five ladies from their restraints. Frankie and Teddy positioned Billie for CPR, ready to spring into action. Just as they were about to begin, a glimmer of hope emerged.

"Wait, Teddy," Frankie exclaimed, her voice filled with a mix of relief and excitement. "She's breathing!"

Relieved, Teddy shouted, "Billie, are you okay?" Her voice rang out, filled with concern and determination.

Billie, weakened but alive, nodded in response, her eyes conveying gratitude.

Travis and Deuce arrived at the property, their car screeching to a halt. With Blue and Cydney in the backseat, they assessed the situation. Deuce called for backup while Travis contemplated how to breach the gated community.

Travis, determined to get inside, made a bold decision. Without hesitation, he accelerated towards the gate, crashing through it, leaving a trail of destruction in their wake. They approached the pool house, ready to rescue their loved ones.

As Travis ran towards the pool house, he stumbles over a man on the ground, unconscious. He checks for a pulse. The man is still breathing. Travis is relieved and continue running towards the flames.

Inside the basement, Bikori and the ladies devised a plan to escape. However, they faced a locked door with no key in sight. In a desperate act,

Bikori threw his body against the door, repeatedly slamming into it. Charlie, consumed by fear, urged them to hurry.

With relentless determination, Bikori kicked and kicked until the door finally gave way. They burst through, relieved to find freedom within reach. Bikori took charge, assigning Teddy and Frankie to assist Billie while he aided Charlie and Suni.

The group worked swiftly, united by a shared goal. Each woman made it out of the basement, their survival a testament to their resilience. Bikori and Charlie reunited in an embrace and expressed their love and remorse amidst the chaos and destruction.

As they caught their breath, Bikori noticed flashing lights and heard the approaching sirens. His gaze shifted from Charlie to the top of the hill. He reassured her that help was on the way. However, a sense of farewell lingered in the air.

Bikori bid his final goodbye, running back into the burning house. Charlie, overcome with grief and desperation, tried to break free from Teddy's grasp. But Teddy, determined to protect her, held on tightly, providing comfort and support.

The sound of approaching sirens grew louder, signaling the arrival of the authorities. Travis searched for Frankie, their voices calling out to one another amidst the chaos. They found each other, tears streaming down their faces, and sought solace in each other's arms.

Cydney, witnessing the reunion, reached out to Teddy and embraced her with relief. Her concern extended to Charlie, offering her support and consolation during this trying moment. Suni, too, found comfort as she was reunited with Blue.

Together, they made their way up the hill, guided by the sound of the sirens. Their hearts pounded with a mix of relief and anguish. As they walked, the pool house collapsed behind them, reducing their former prison to rubble.

Charlie turned around, her eyes fixed on the smoldering ruins. Overwhelmed by the devastation, she let out a piercing scream. Teddy, holding her tightly, reassured her that they would be okay, providing a sense of strength and solace.

Fade out.

Months later, Charlie and the ladies found themselves in front of the Bellman's Cemetery once again. Memories flooded their minds as they gathered around. Teddy broke the silence, acknowledging the familiarity of the situation.

Frankie chimed in, acknowledging the strange sense of déjà vu. Billie offered her support, asking if Charlie needed them to accompany her. Charlie, a glimmer of a smile on her face, declined their offer, expressing her gratitude.

As Charlie stepped out of the car and began to walk, a sense of determination enveloped her. With her head held high, she forged ahead, ready to confront her past and embrace her future, leaving the ashes behind.

Charlie stood before Bikori's grave, overwhelmed by a mix of grief and love. Tears streamed down her face as she poured out her heart, expressing her pain and longing for him. The weight of her emotions bore heavily upon her as she placed red roses on Bikori's tombstone.

"I knew this would be hard, but I had no idea how hard," Charlie sobbed, her voice choked with emotion. "Sorry I haven't come sooner. A part of me has yet to let you go. There were days I wished I had gone back into that house with you. In my heart, we were one, and when you died, a part of me died that day. I felt like life was not worth living without you. I'm glad you were able to see the good in me despite the circumstances. Thank you for forgiving me." Her words trembled with a mix of sorrow and gratitude.

As she bent over to place the roses on Bikori's grave, Charlie's gaze shifted to Brandy's tombstone, a surge of emotion coursing through her. She took a rose from the bouquet and laid it before Brandy's resting place, a gesture of honor and acknowledgment for the connection they shared. With a heavy heart, Charlie returned to Bikori's grave, standing tall before it.

Her tear-filled eyes closed, and she blew a final kiss to Bikori. "I love you, babe," she whispered, her voice breaking. Standing there with closed eyes, Charlie took a deep breath, feeling a mix of pain and solace. "Yeah, I can dream," she said softly to herself, finding a flicker of hope amidst the darkness.

Startled by a sudden crash, rumble, and the deafening sound of thunder, Charlie's eyes popped open, her heart racing. Looking up at the sky, she saw rain pouring down, transforming into hail. An urgency filled her as she realized she needed to get home.

However, to her surprise, she found herself unable to move her feet. Confusion and fear gripped her as she looked down at the ground. Something held her in place, an invisible force keeping her rooted to the spot. Panic surged through her veins as she attempted to pry herself free, her hands desperately grasping at her ankles.

"What the... why can't I move my feet?" Charlie's voice quivered with a mix of disbelief and terror. She struggled, tugging at her ankles, but the grip only tightened, pulling her closer to the ground. Her pleas for help turned into screams, echoing through the air.

"Please, somebody help me!" Charlie's voice cracked with desperation, her eyes scanning the surroundings for any sign of assistance. But her cries fell on deaf ears, drowned out by the storm raging around her. She fought with all her might, clawing at the ground, but the force pulling her under grew stronger, its hold unyielding.

Gasping for breath, Charlie suddenly awoke in a hospital bed, her body drenched in sweat. Her eyes darted around the room, registering the presence of her loved ones. Her mother, father, Tee Tee, Bella, and all four ladies stood by her side, their faces etched with concern.

"It's okay, baby," her mother's soothing voice reached her ears. "You were having a nightmare. We're here for you, and everything will be okay." Her mother's embrace offered a sense of comfort and safety.

Charlie clung to her daughter Bella, who laid her head on Charlie's lap. Teddy, with tears in her eyes, reached out to hold Charlie's trembling hand. "We've got you, sis," Teddy's voice quivered with empathy and reassurance.

Overwhelmed with relief, Charlie reached out her arms, her eyes filled with tears. "Go get him," she pleaded, her voice barely a whisper. The room fell silent, and Suni, understanding Charlie's unspoken request, quietly left the room.

Moments later, Suni returned, accompanied by a nurse pushing a small Isolate. Inside lay a baby boy, his tiny form nestled in blankets. As the nurse carefully placed the baby in Charlie's arms, a wave of emotion washed over her. She held him close, her tears falling freely.

"He's beautiful," Charlie managed to say between sobs. The baby's presence filled her with a sense of hope and new beginnings.

Surrounded by her family, Charlie found solace and comfort in their presence. They assured her that everything would be okay, that they were there to support and love her unconditionally. Charlie closed her eyes, allowing herself to bask in the warmth of their love.

Outside her hospital room, a figure stood by a tree, wearing a hooded sweatshirt. The person's gaze was fixed upon Charlie's window, a mixture of relief and tenderness in their eyes. Without uttering a word, they turned and walked away, disappearing into the distance.

The closing chapter concluded with Deuce, known as Roman Lamont Johnston Jr., stepping forward as the narrator. He expresses deep sorrow and empathy for what happened to Brandy, suggesting that she didn't deserve the pain she endured. He acknowledged the transformative power of words and the impact they can have on a person's life. Deuce urged readers to learn from Charlie's journey, to embrace empathy and acceptance, and to recognize the profound effect our words and actions can have on others.

NATIONAL SUICIDE 24-HOUR HOTLINES

If you or someone you know is experiencing suicidal thoughts or feelings of despair, it's essential to reach out for help immediately.

Please don't hesitate to call a suicide prevention hotline in your country. Trained professionals are available 24/7 to listen, support, and provide valuable resources.

CALL

National Suicide Prevention Lifeline

1-800-273-8255 (1-800-273-TALK)

Veterans in crisis, please press "1" to be directed to local VA resources

En Español, call 1-888-628-9454

TEXT

Crisis Text Line

Text HOME to 741-741

ABOUT THE AUTHOR

Felicia Taylor is a dedicated nurse, devoted mother of three, and proud grandmother of six beautiful grandchildren. Felicia is from St. Louis, Missouri – the 'show me' state, home of the Redd Foxx, Nelly, and Jason Tatum.

Felicia has always had a secret world of storytelling brewing within her. Throughout her busy life, juggling the demands of her career and the joys of motherhood, Felicia often found solace in her imagination, spinning intricate tales in her mind. However, she had never written anything down; these stories existed solely within the depths of her thoughts.

One memorable day, Felicia found herself at the iconic Chinese theater in Hollywood, where she sat mesmerized, watching the timeless classic "Grease" starring Johns Travolta and Olivia Newton-John, not just once but three times in a row.

As she immersed herself in the vibrant world of the movie, Felicia couldn't help but be captivated by Olivia Newton John's Character transformed throughout the film, from shy and innocent to confident and empowered. His transformation resonated deeply within Felicia.

In that moment, she felt a profound connection to Olivia Newton John's portrayal, and a seed was planted in her heart. She knew then and there that she wanted to be a part of the world of storytelling and entertainment.

Felicia Taylor's decision to embark on her writing journey later in life serves as a testament to the enduring nature of dreams and the importance of embracing one's creative calling. Her story is a reminder that it is never too late to pursue one's passions and have faith that there are readers who consistently get touched by the stories we have to tell.